OTTO'S ORANGE DAY

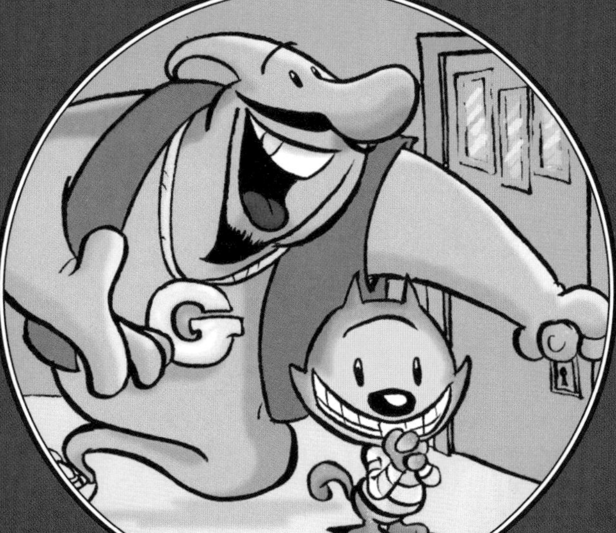

A TOON BOOK BY

JAY LYNCH & FRANK CAMMUSO

AN IMPRINT OF CANDLEWICK PRESS

OOKLIST'S TOP 10 GRAPHIC NOVELS FOR YOUTH
ALA'S CORE COLLECTION OF GRAPHIC NOVELS
HIC NOVEL REPORTER'S CORE LIST OF GN FOR KIDS
ALSC'S BEST GRAPHIC NOVELS FOR CHILDREN

Also look for OTTO'S BACKWARDS DAY, by the same authors.

For Ngoc
–Frank

For Kathleen and Norah
–Jay

Editorial Director: FRANÇOISE MOULY

Book Design: FRANÇOISE MOULY & JONATHAN BENNETT

FRANK CAMMUSO'S artwork is drawn in ink and colored digitally.

A TOON Book™ © 2008 RAW Junior, LLC, 27 Greene Street, New York, NY 10013. TOON Books is an imprint of Candlewick Press, 99 Dover Street, Somerville, MA 02144. No part of this book may be used or reproduced in any manner whatsoever without written permission except in the case of brief quotations embodied in critical articles and reviews. TOON Books®, LITTLE LIT® and TOON into Reading!™ are trademarks of RAW Junior, LLC. All rights reserved. Printed in Johor Bahru, Malaysia.

Library of Congress Control Number: 2007941868

ISBN 13: 978-0-9799238-2-1 ISBN 10: 0-9799238-2-4

13 14 15 16 17 18 TWP 10 9 8 7 6 5 4

WWW.TOON-BOOKS.COM

CHAPTER ONE:

MY
FAVORITE
COLOR!

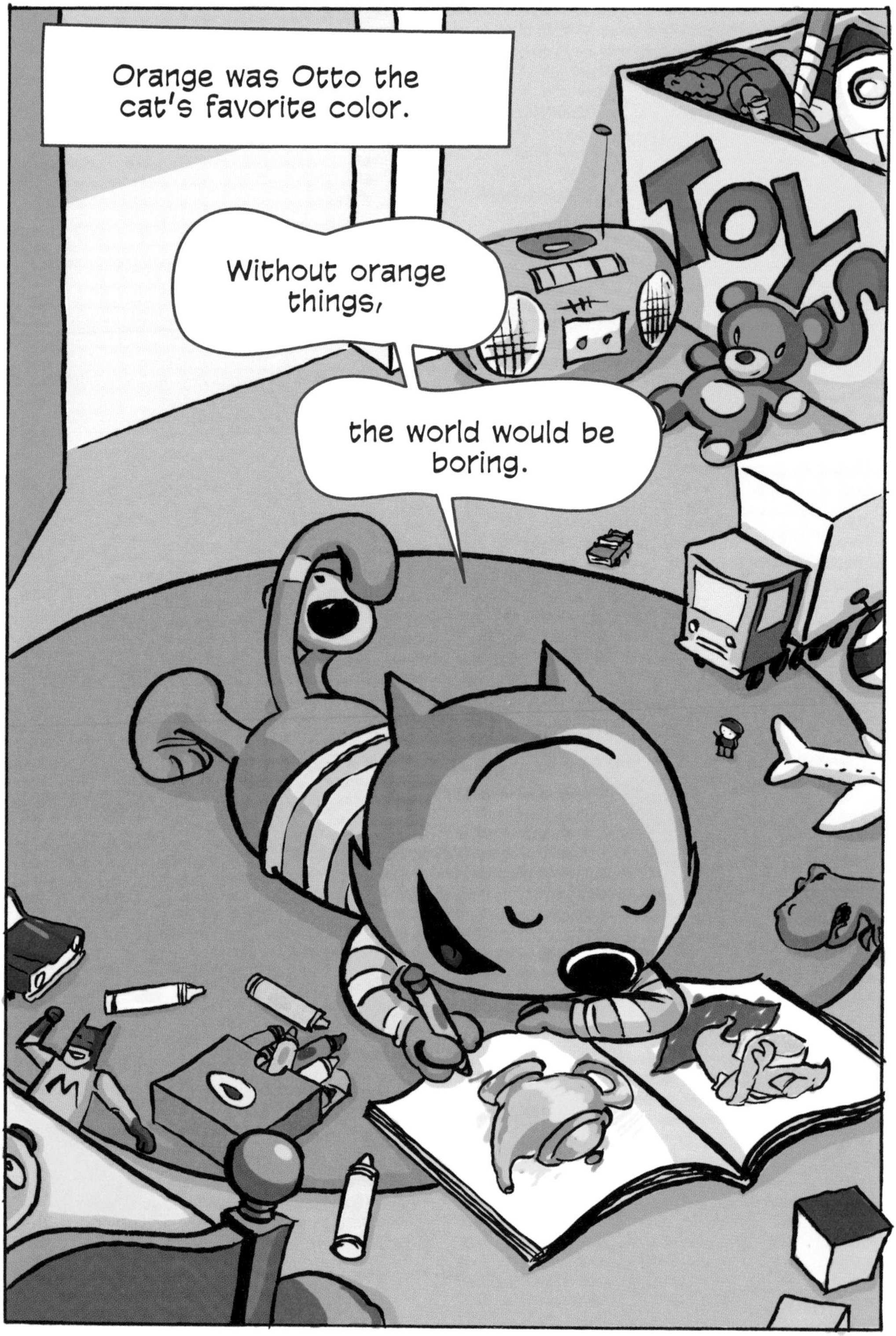
Orange was Otto the cat's favorite color.
Without orange things,
the world would be boring.
TOYS

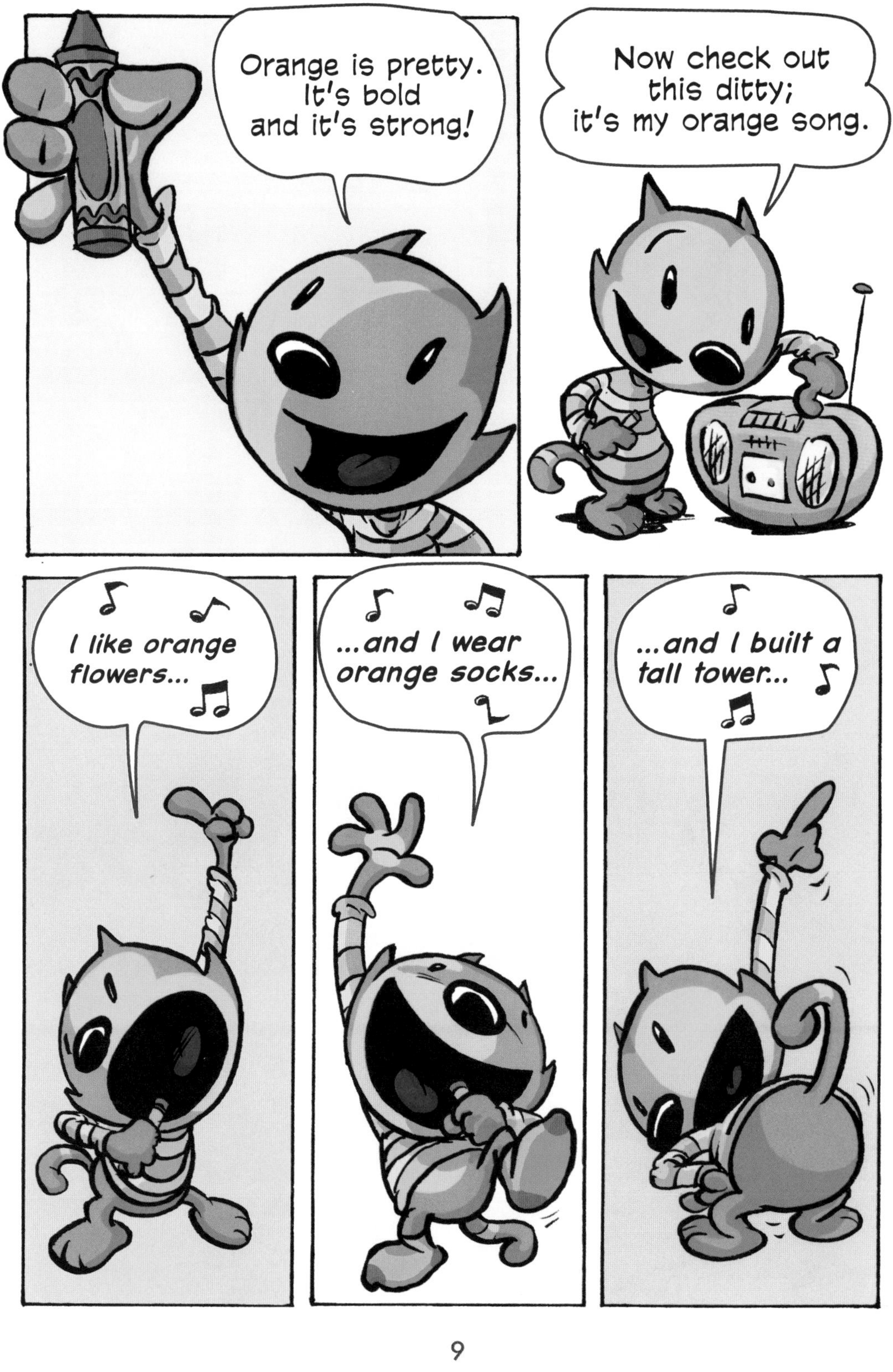
Orange is pretty. It's bold and it's strong!
Now check out this ditty; it's my orange song.
I like orange flowers...
...and I wear orange socks...
...and I built a tall tower...

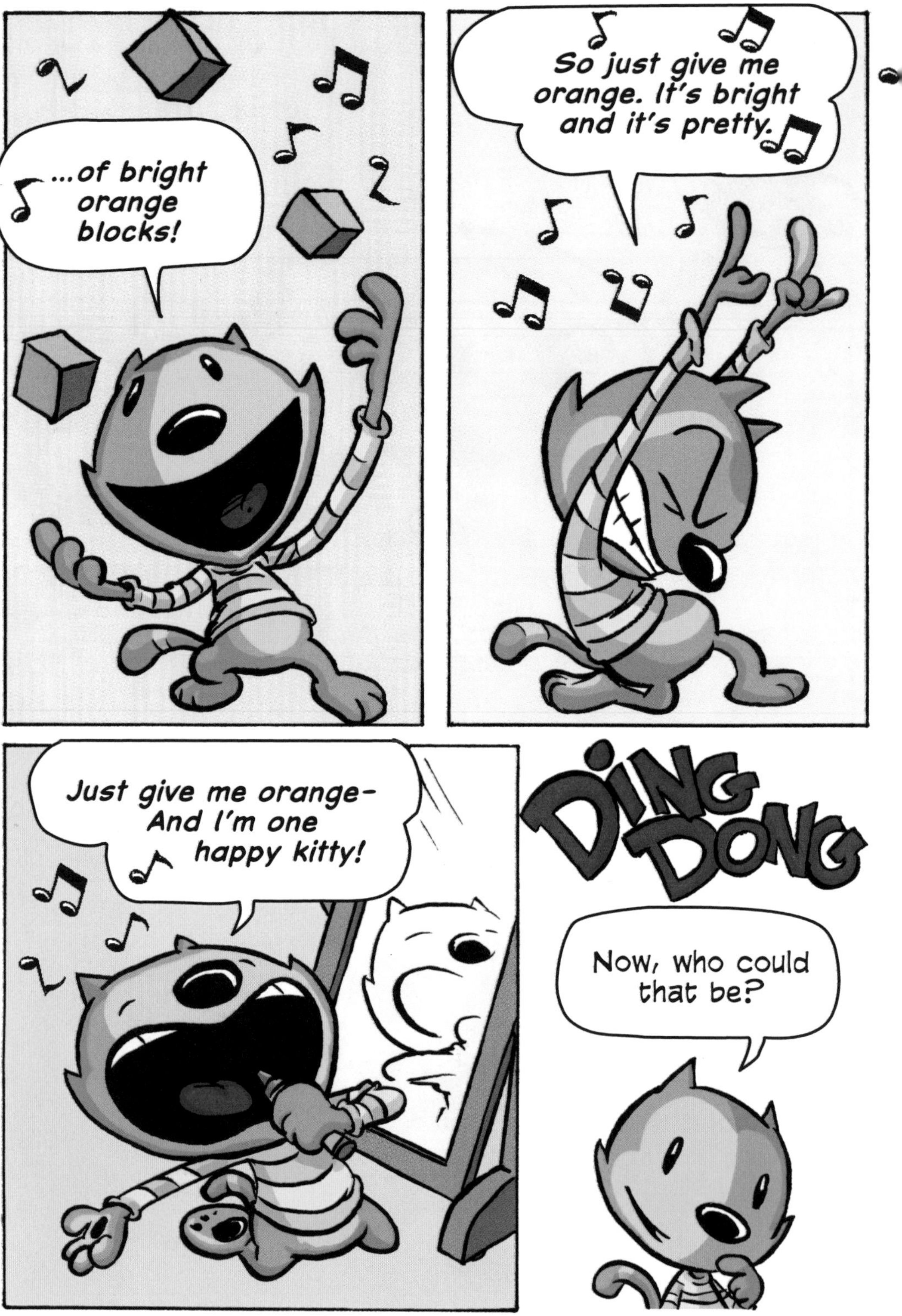
...of bright orange blocks!
So just give me orange. It's bright and it's pretty.
Just give me orange- And I'm one happy kitty!
DING DONG
Now, who could that be?

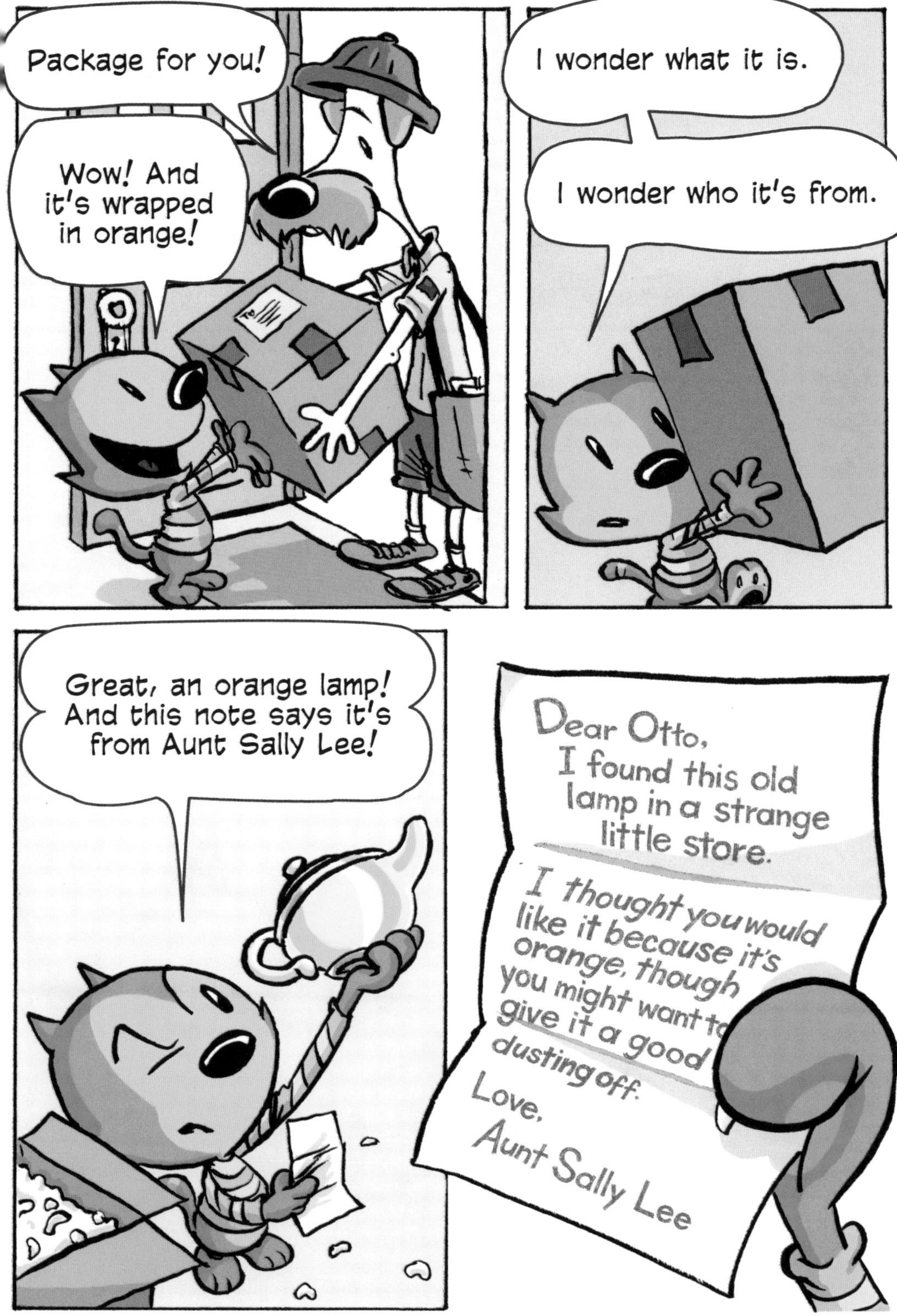
Package for you!
Wow! And it's wrapped in orange!
I wonder what it is.
I wonder who it's from.
Great, an orange lamp! And this note says it's from Aunt Sally Lee!
Dear Otto,
I found this old lamp in a strange little store.
I thought you would like it because it's orange, though you might want to give it a good dusting off.
Love,
Aunt Sally Lee

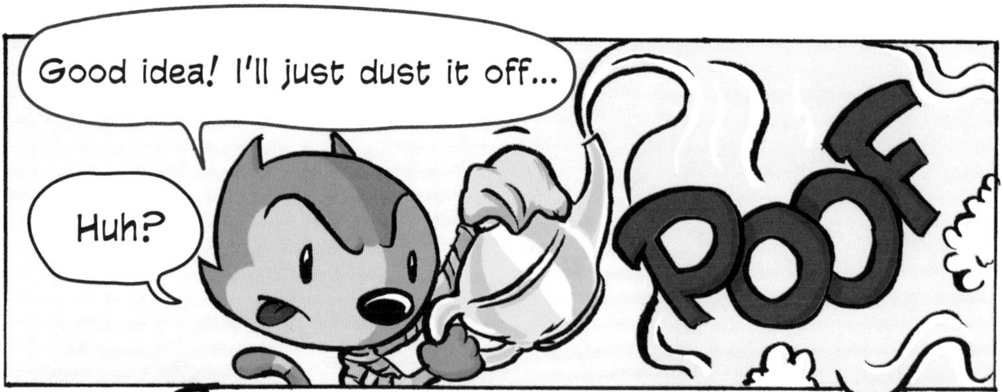
Good idea! I'll just dust it off...
Huh?
POOF

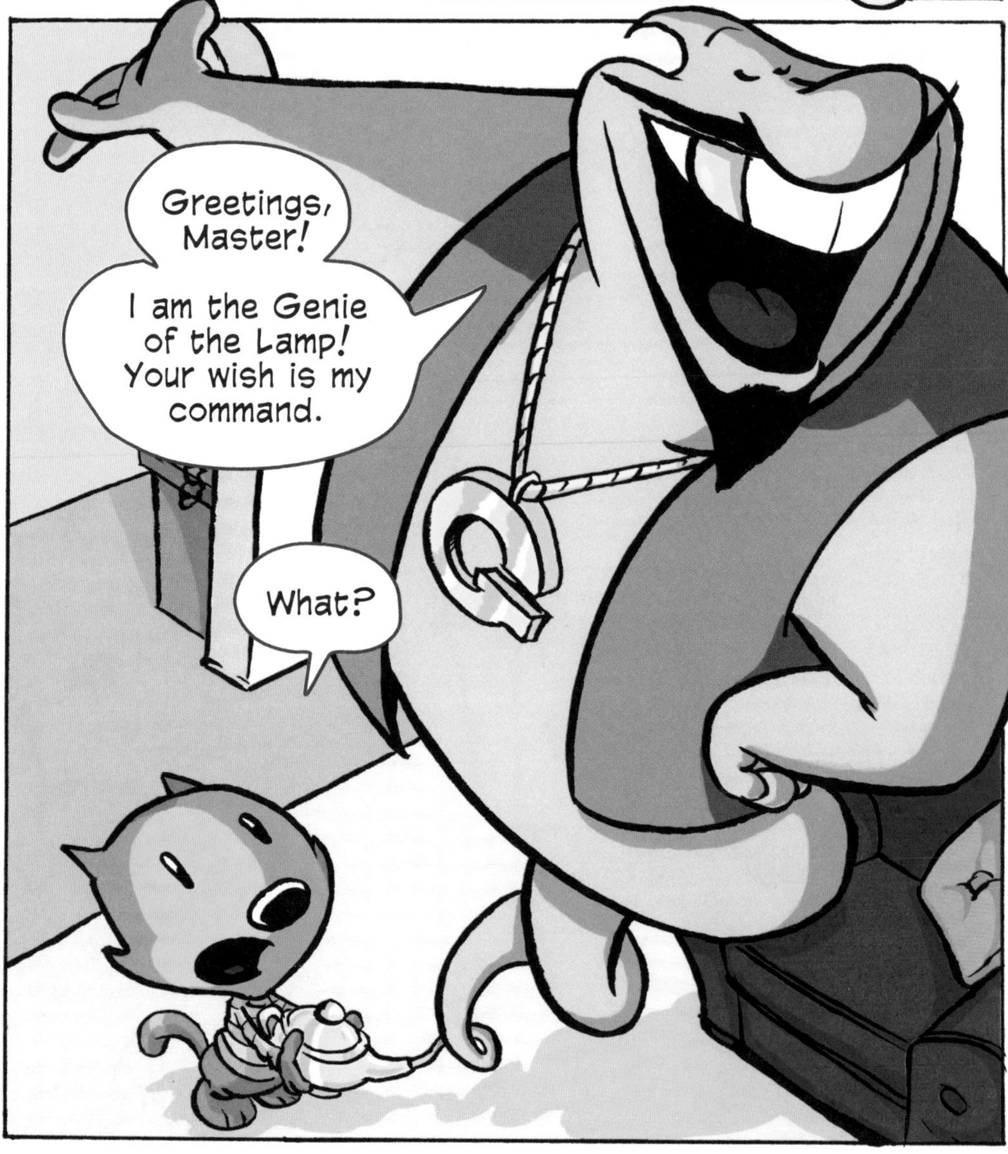
Greetings, Master!
I am the Genie of the Lamp! Your wish is my command.
What?

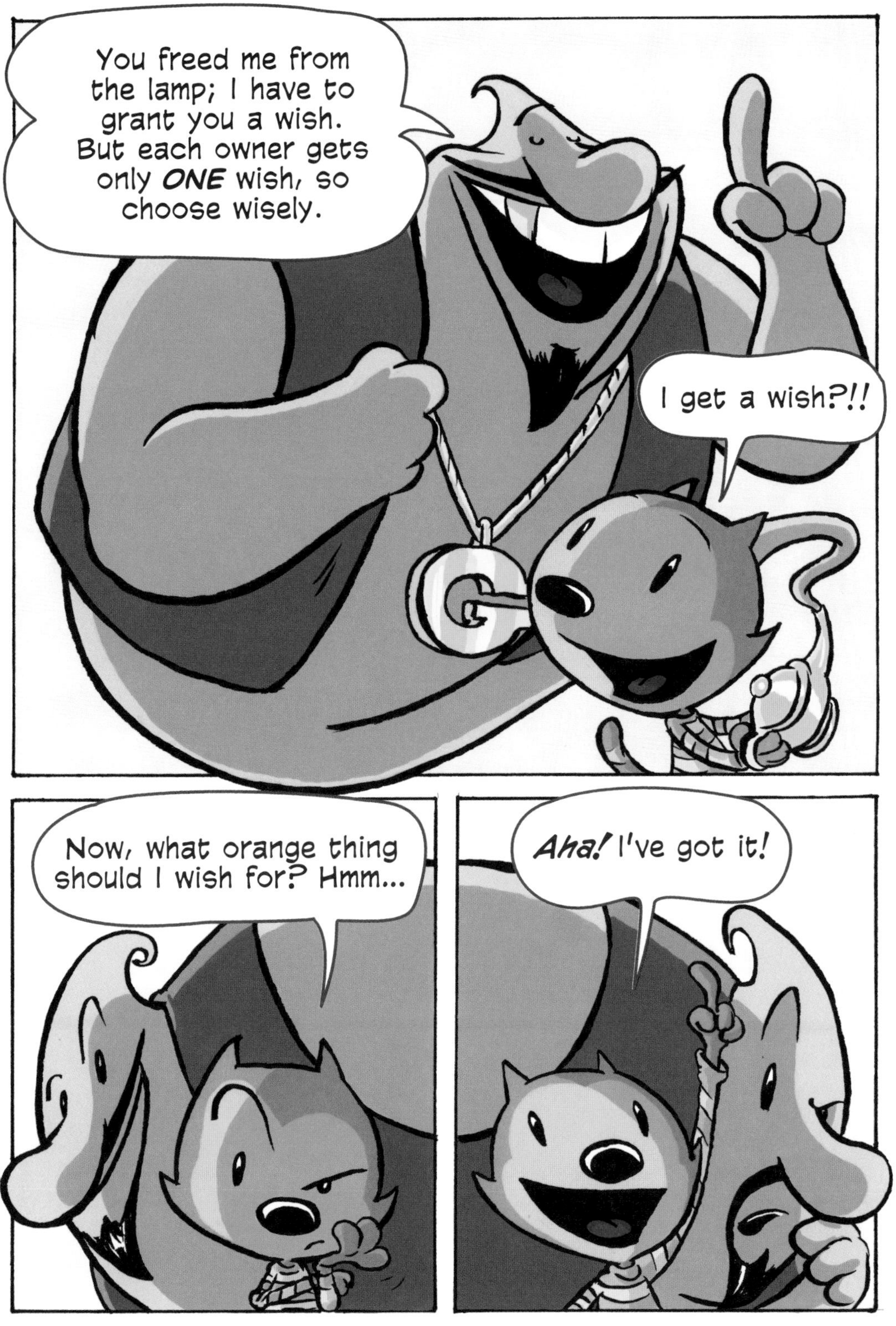
You freed me from the lamp; I have to grant you a wish. But each owner gets only ONE wish, so choose wisely.
I get a wish?!!
Now, what orange thing should I wish for? Hmm...
Aha! I've got it!

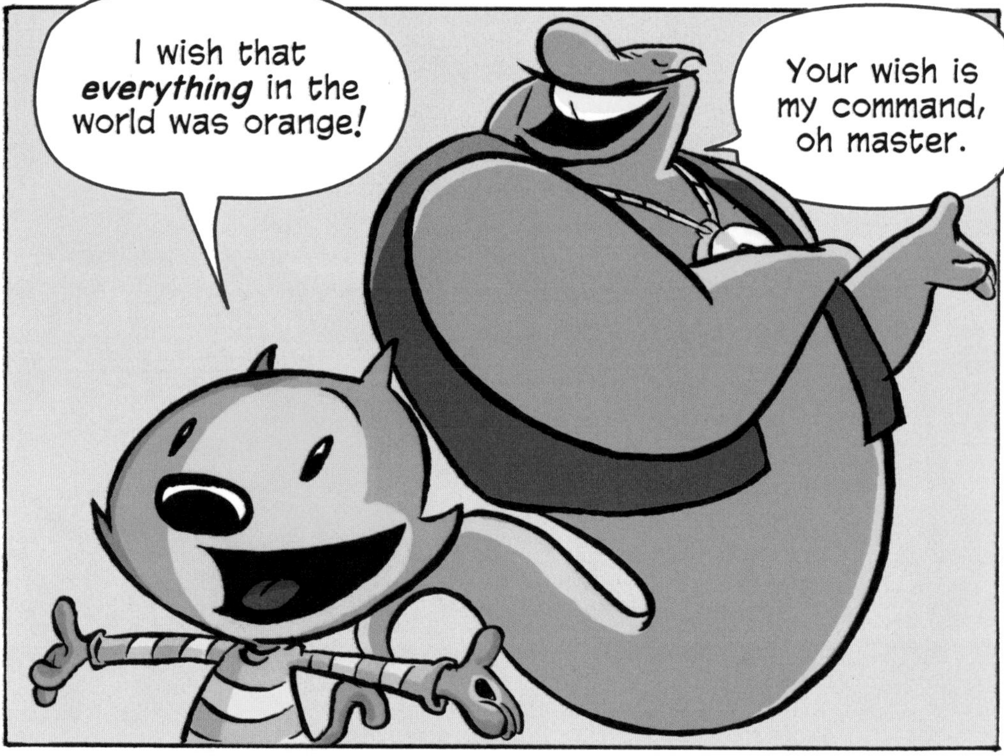
I wish that *everything* in the world was orange!
Your wish is my command, oh master.

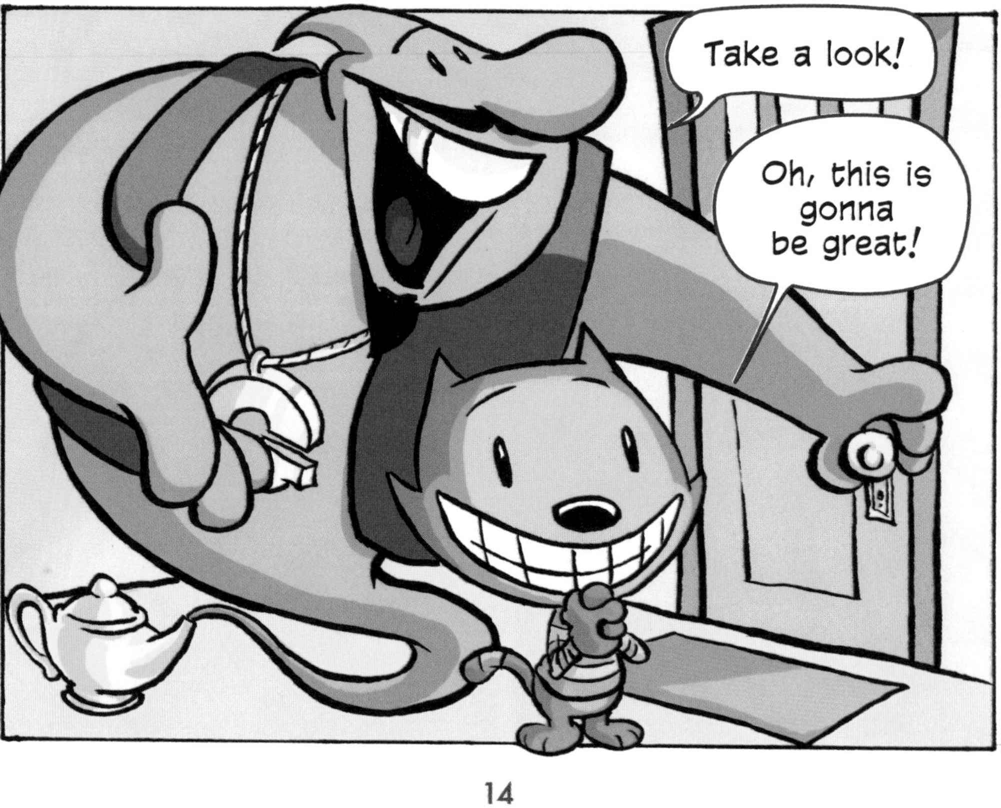
Take a look!
Oh, this is gonna be great!

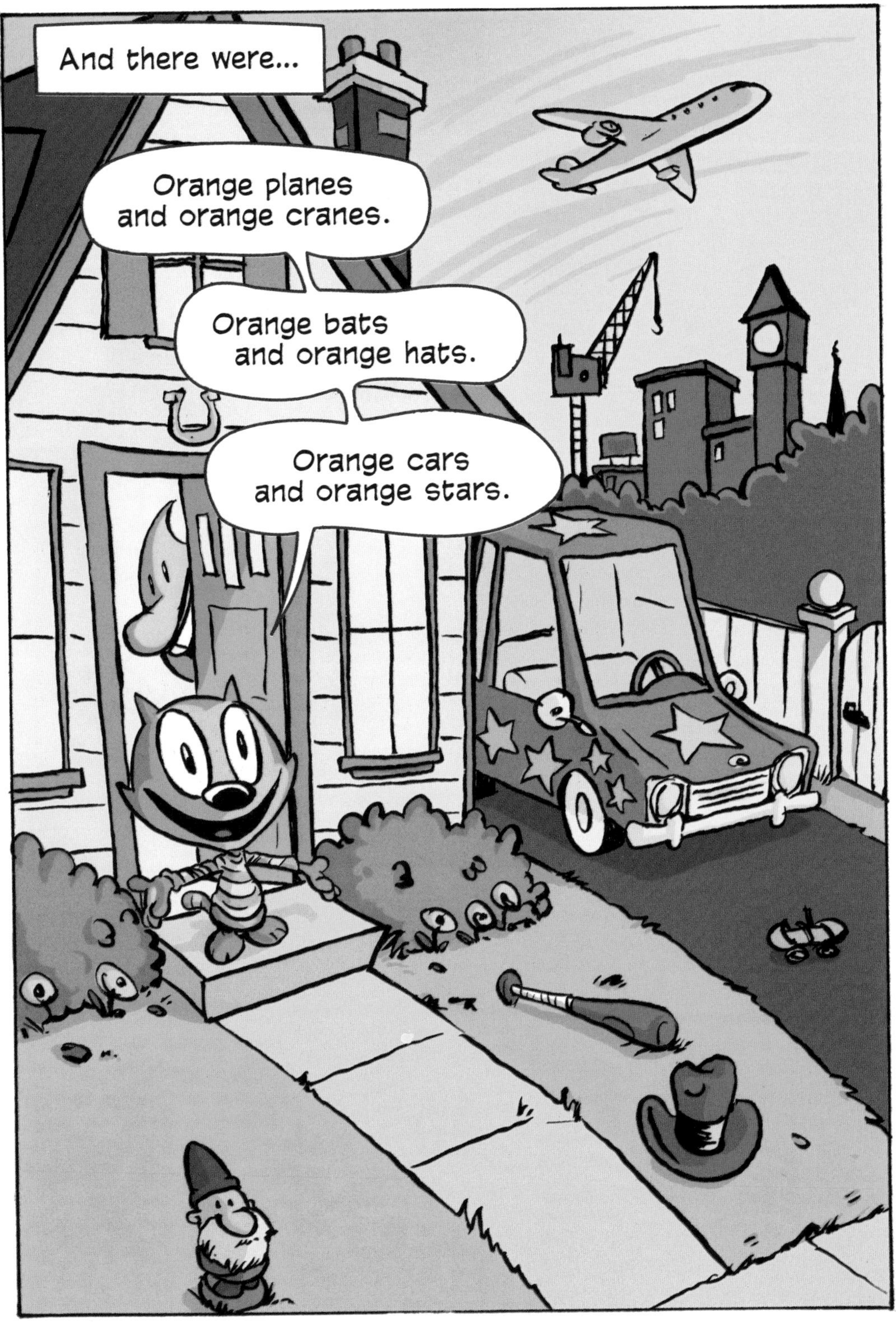
And there were...
Orange planes and orange cranes.
Orange bats and orange hats.
Orange cars and orange stars.

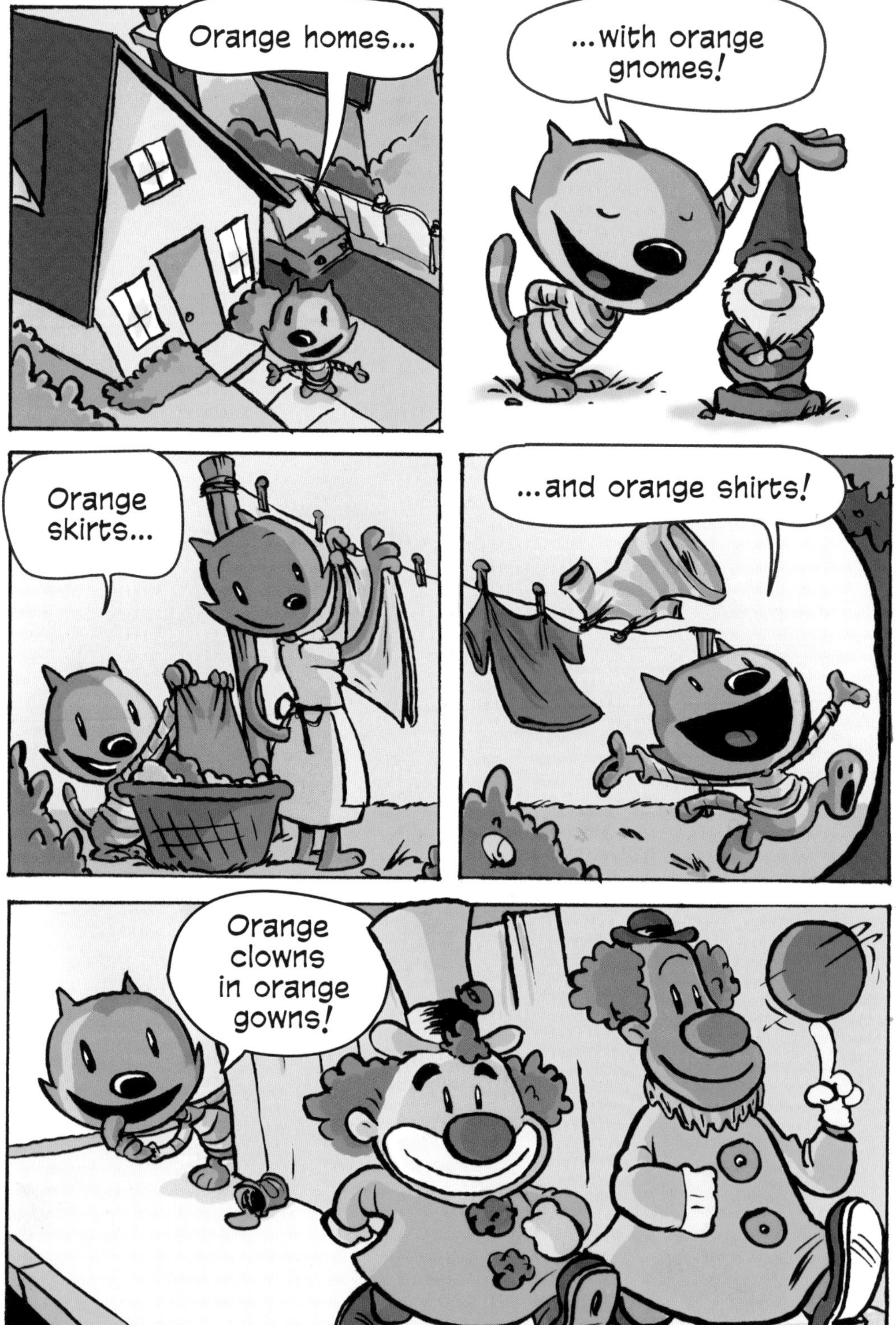
Orange homes...
...with orange gnomes!
Orange skirts...
...and orange shirts!
Orange clowns in orange gowns!

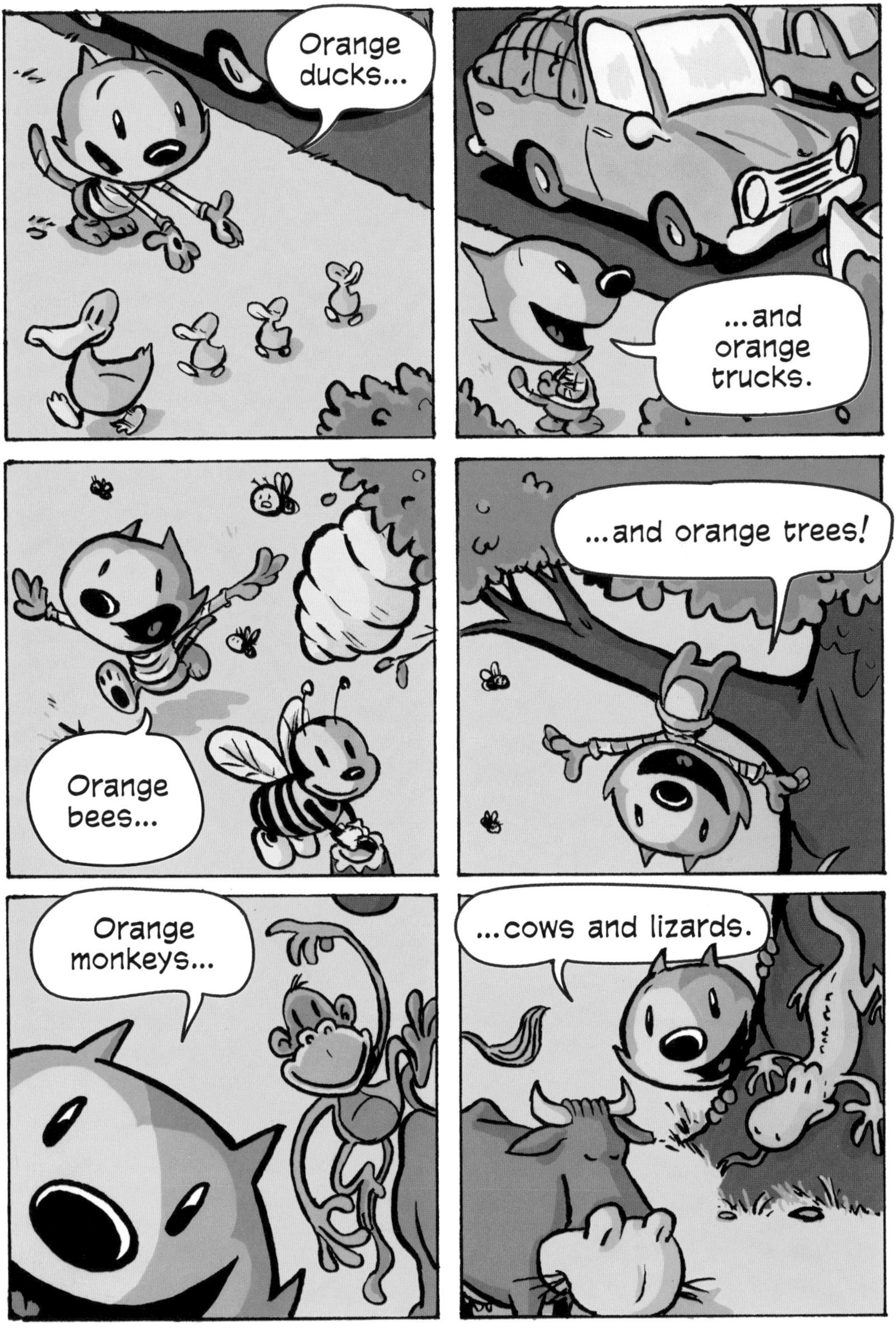
Orange ducks...
...and orange trucks.
Orange bees...
...and orange trees!
Orange monkeys...
...cows and lizards.

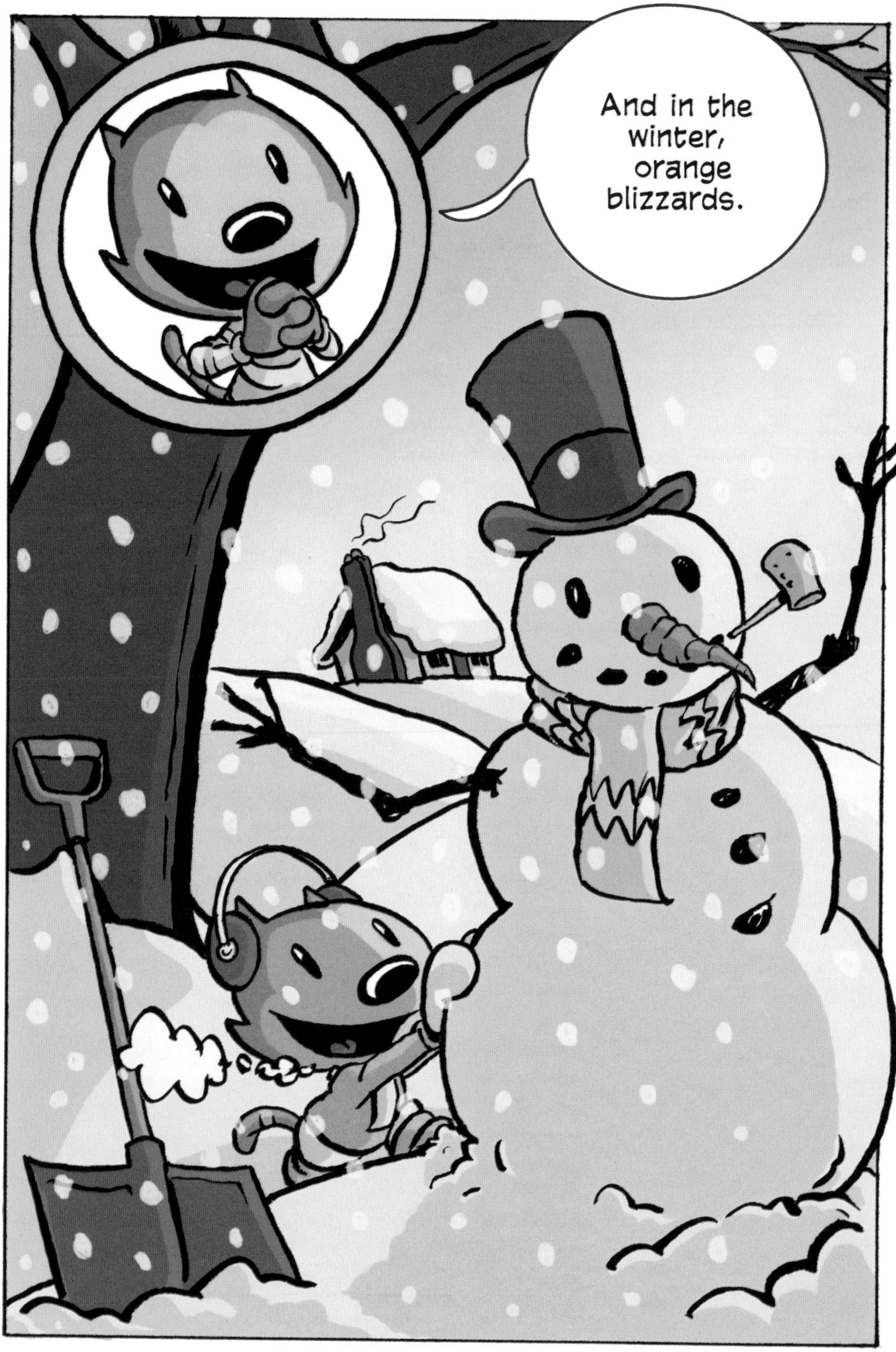
And in the winter, orange blizzards.

CHAPTER TWO:

BE CAREFUL WHAT YOU WISH FOR!

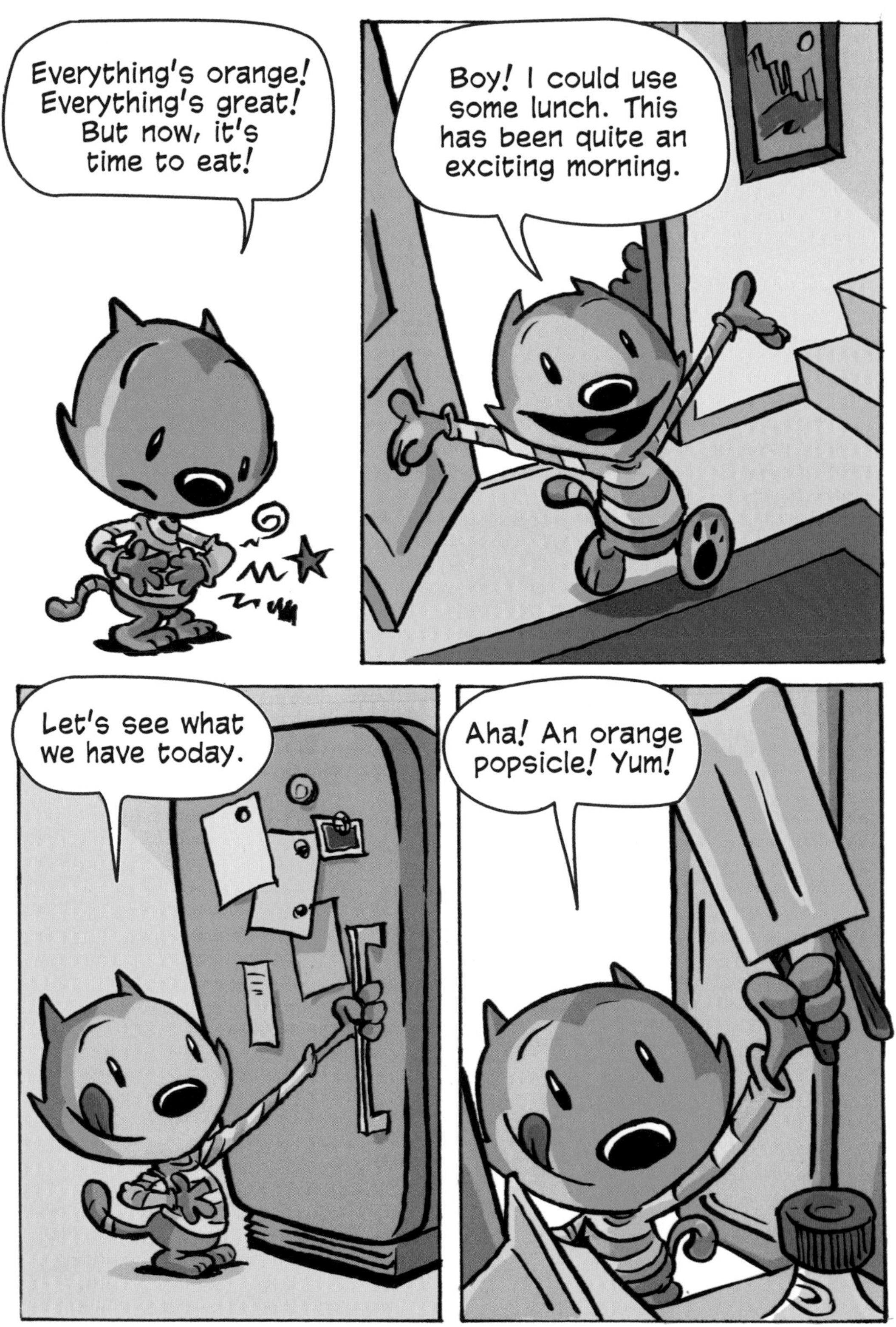
Everything's orange! Everything's great! But now, it's time to eat!
Boy! I could use some lunch. This has been quite an exciting morning.
Let's see what we have today.
Aha! An orange popsicle! Yum!

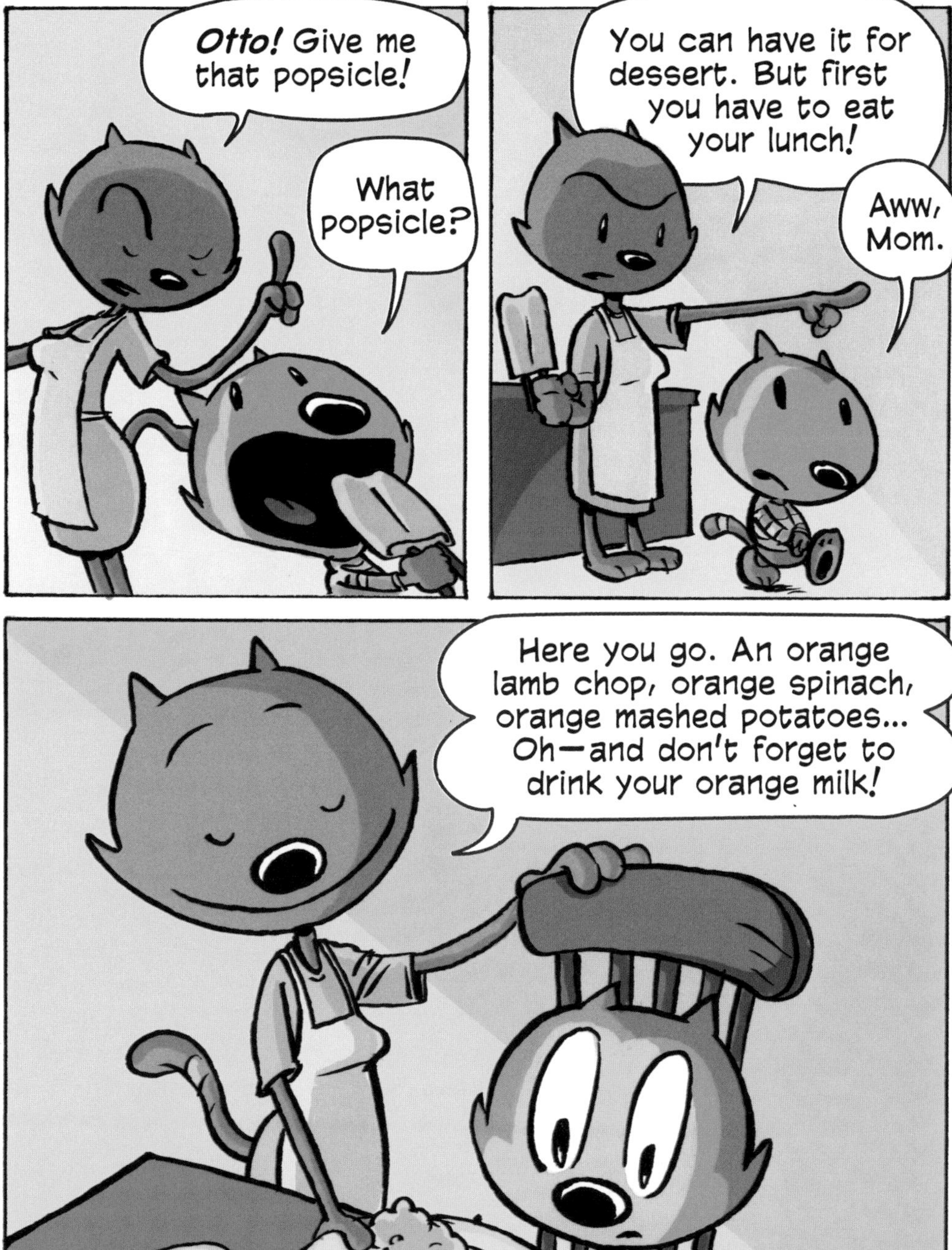
Otto! Give me that popsicle!
What popsicle?
You can have it for dessert. But first you have to eat your lunch!
Aww, Mom.
Here you go. An orange lamb chop, orange spinach, orange mashed potatoes... Oh—and don't forget to drink your orange milk!

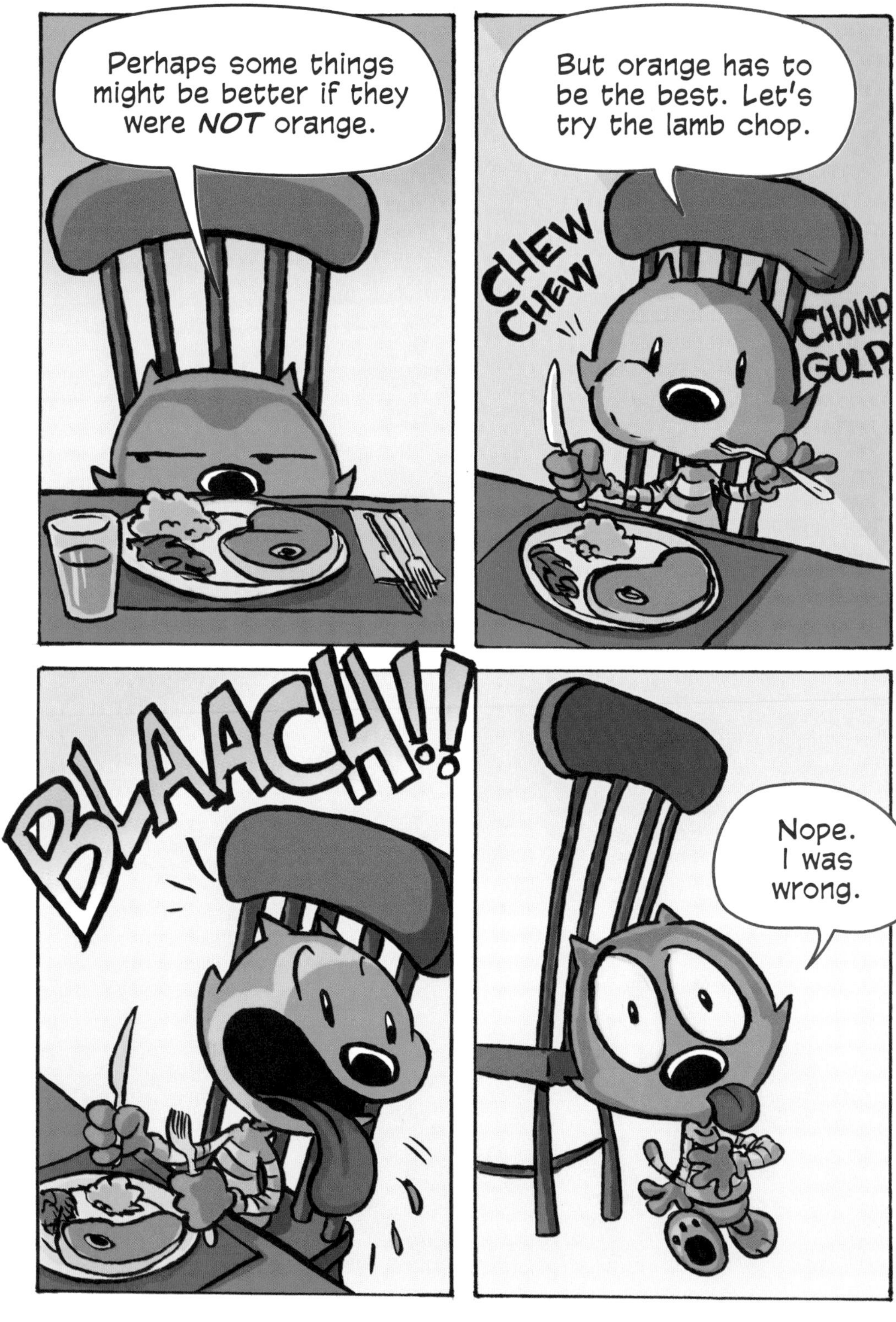
Perhaps some things might be better if they were NOT orange.
But orange has to be the best. Let's try the lamb chop.
CHEW CHEW
CHOMP GULP
BLAACH!!
Nope. I was wrong.

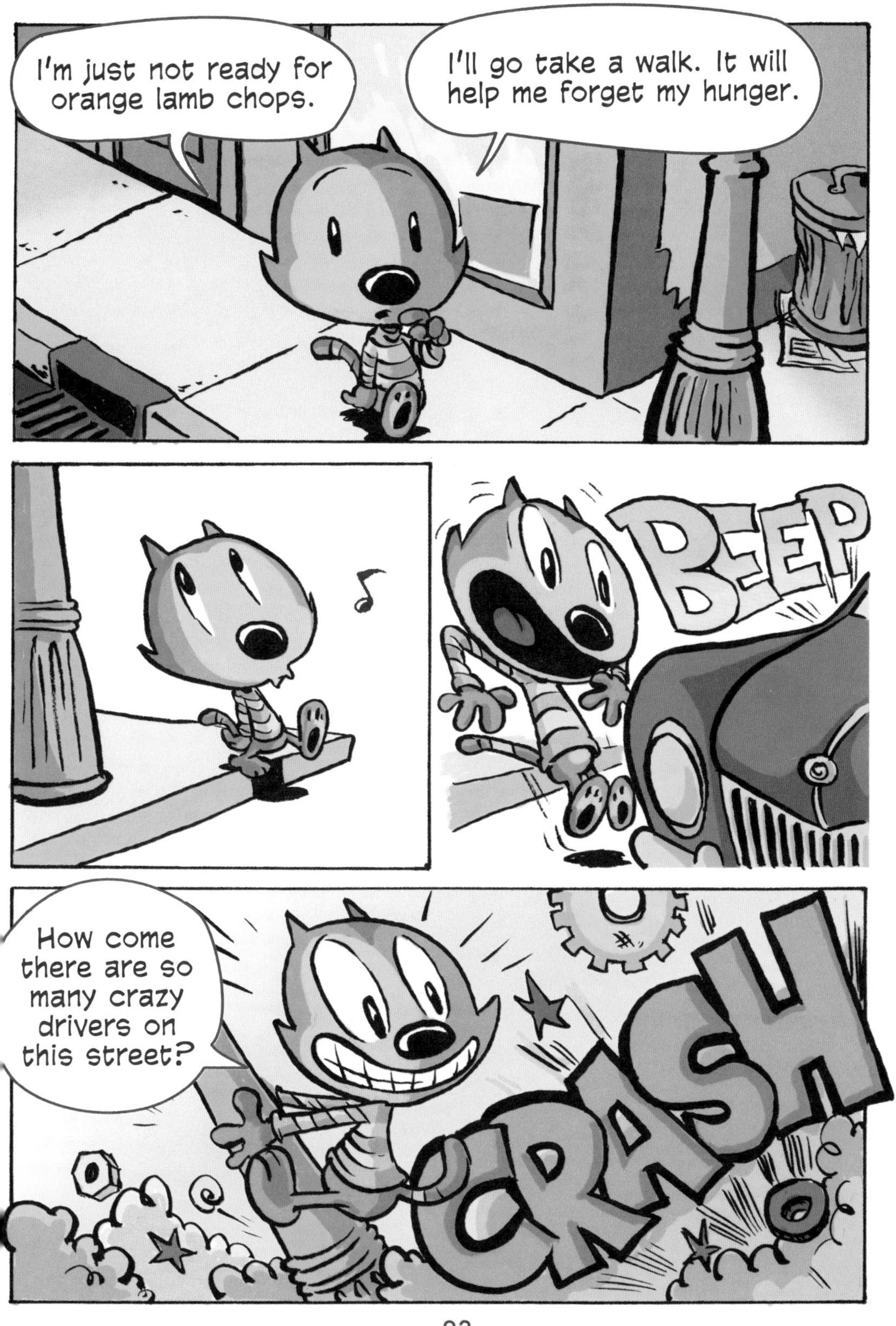
I'm just not ready for orange lamb chops.
I'll go take a walk. It will help me forget my hunger.
BEEP
How come there are so many crazy drivers on this street?
CRASH

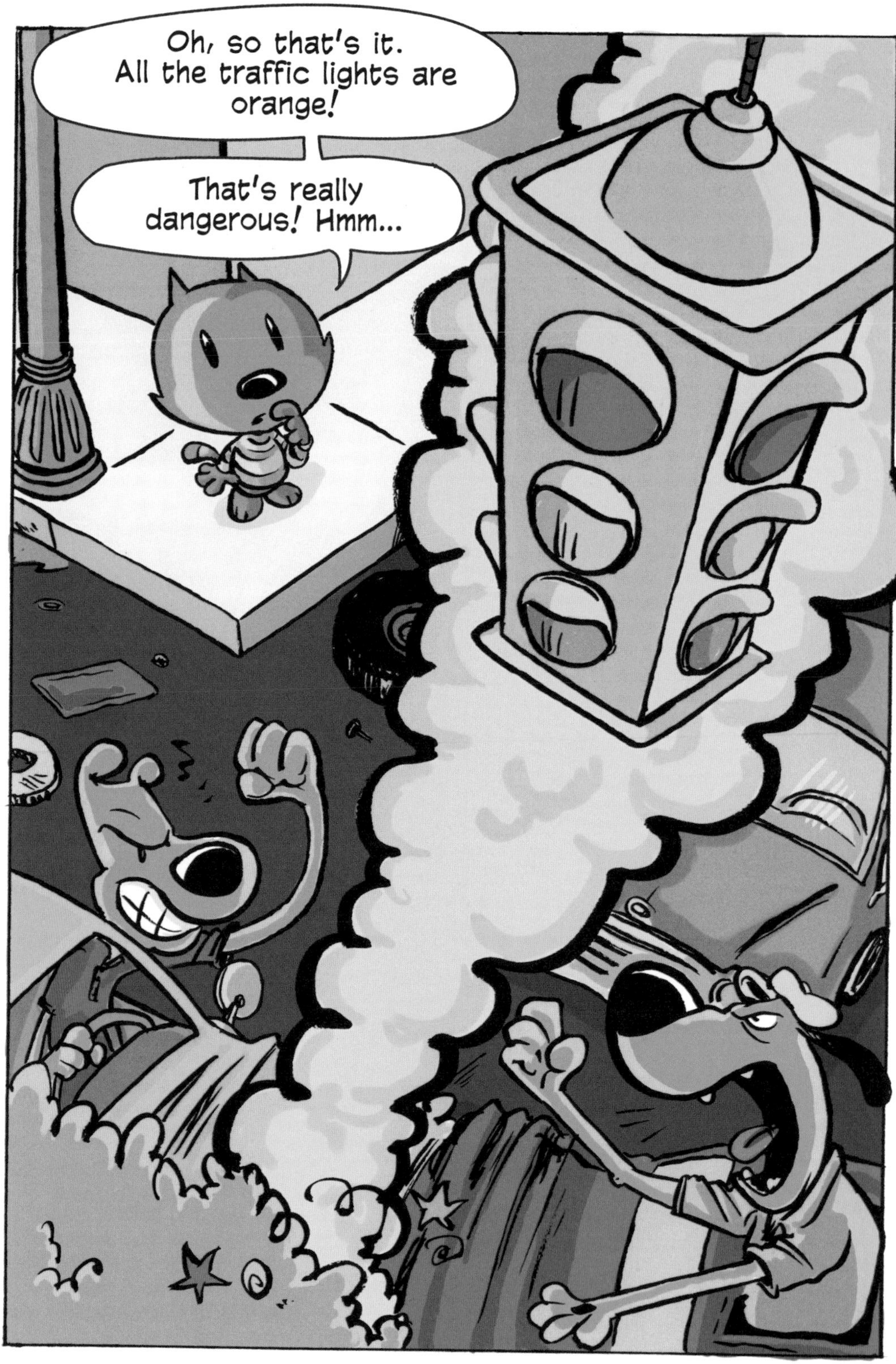
Oh, so that's it. All the traffic lights are orange!
That's really dangerous! Hmm...

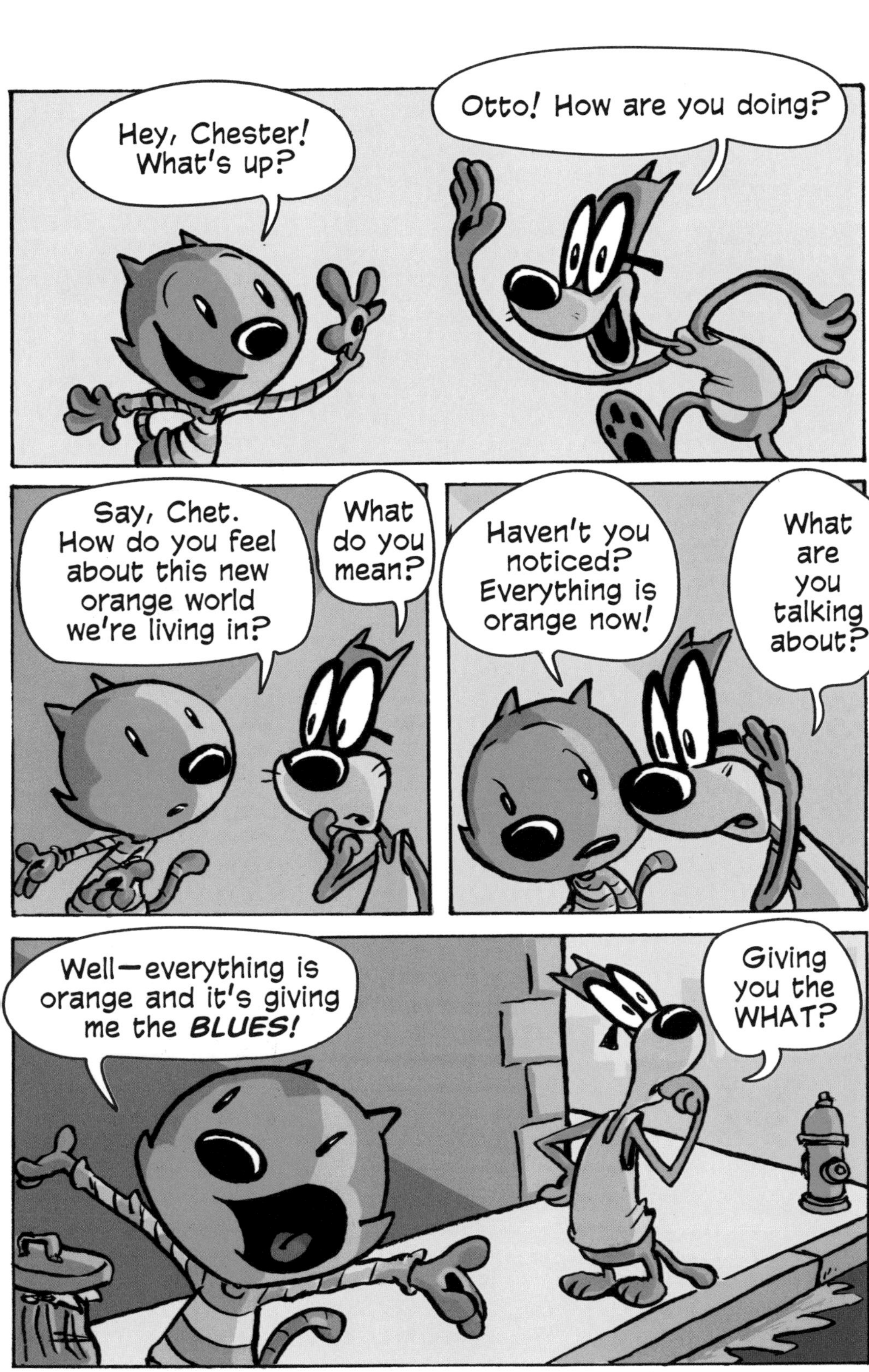
Hey, Chester! What's up?
Otto! How are you doing?
Say, Chet. How do you feel about this new orange world we're living in?
What do you mean?
Haven't you noticed? Everything is orange now!
What are you talking about?
Well—everything is orange and it's giving me the ***BLUES!***
Giving you the WHAT?

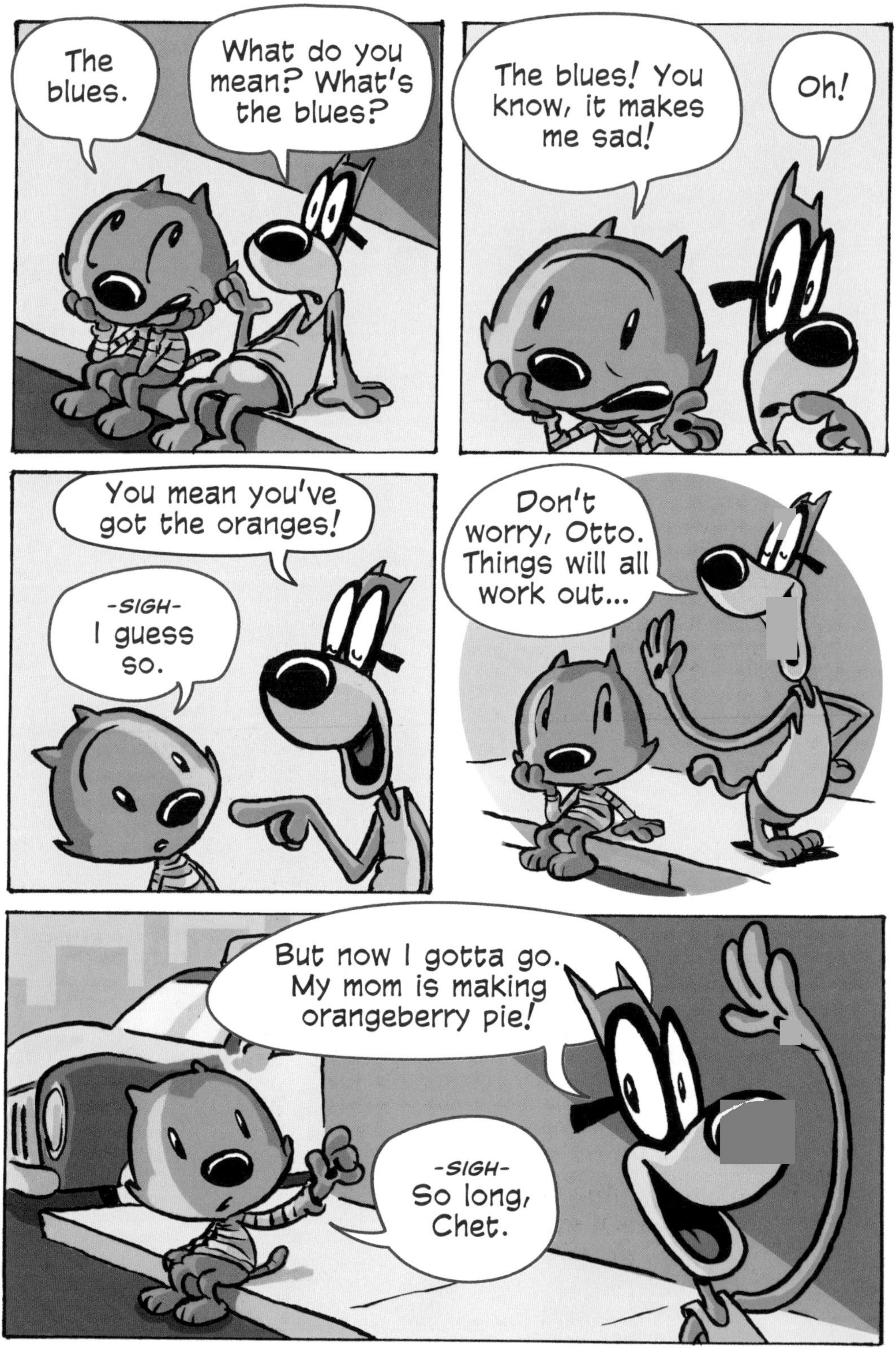
The blues.
What do you mean? What's the blues?
The blues! You know, it makes me sad!
Oh!
You mean you've got the oranges!
-SIGH- I guess so.
Don't worry, Otto. Things will all work out...
But now I gotta go. My mom is making orangeberry pie!
-SIGH- So long, Chet.

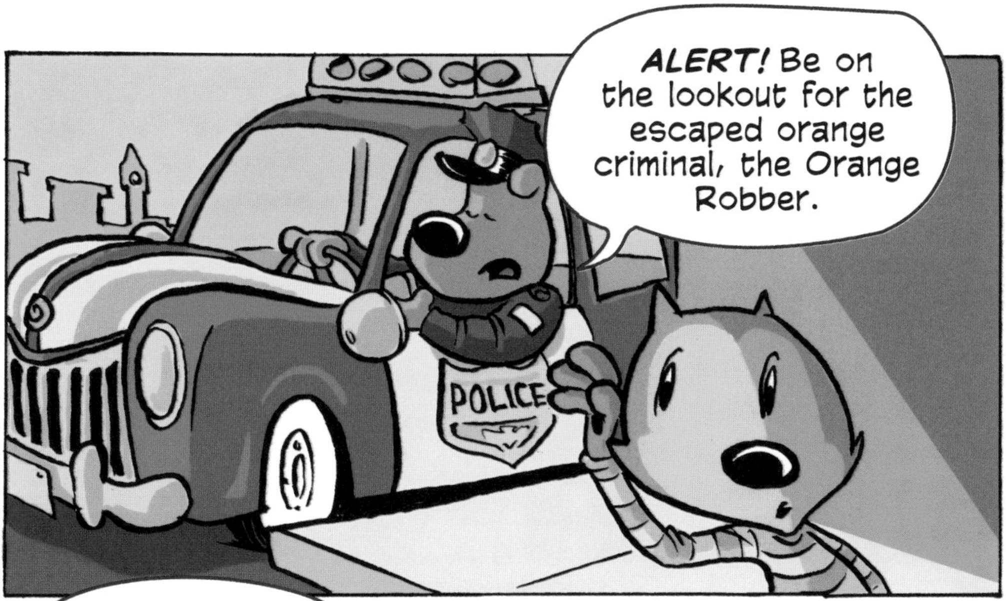
ALERT! Be on the lookout for the escaped orange criminal, the Orange Robber.
POLICE

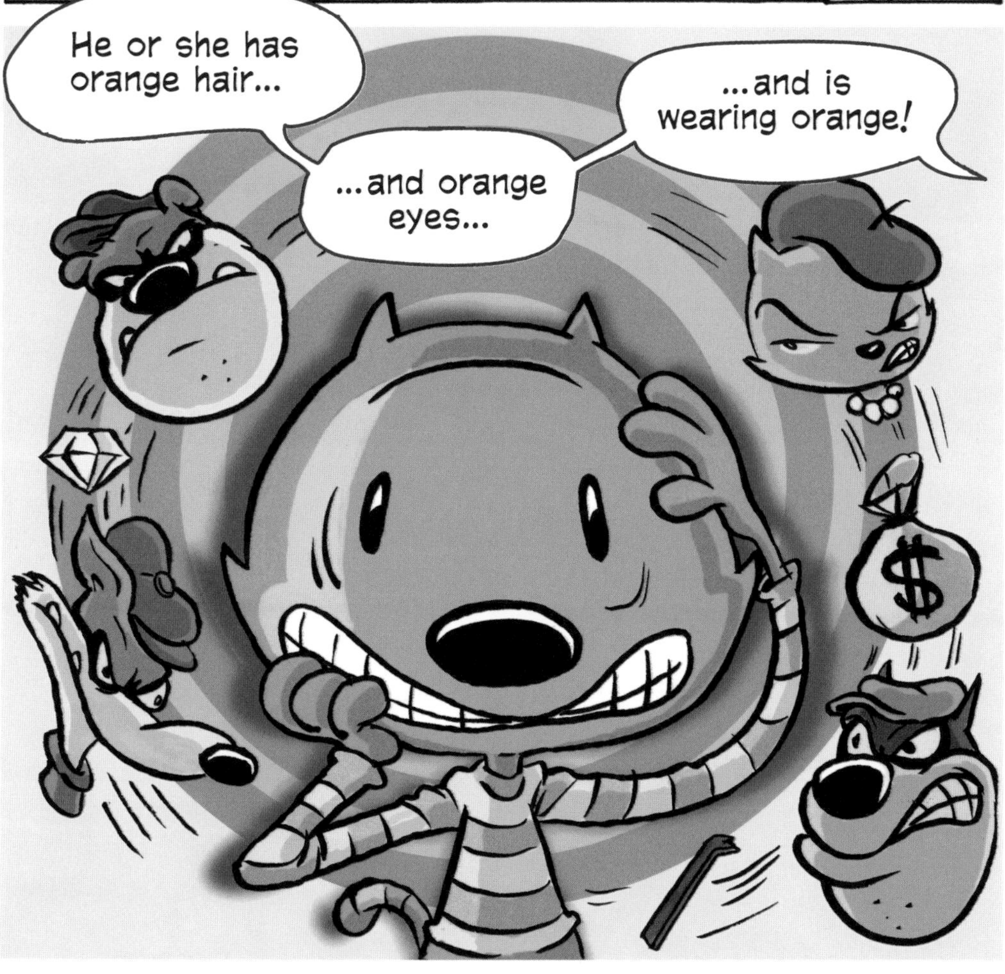
He or she has orange hair...
...and orange eyes...
...and is wearing orange!

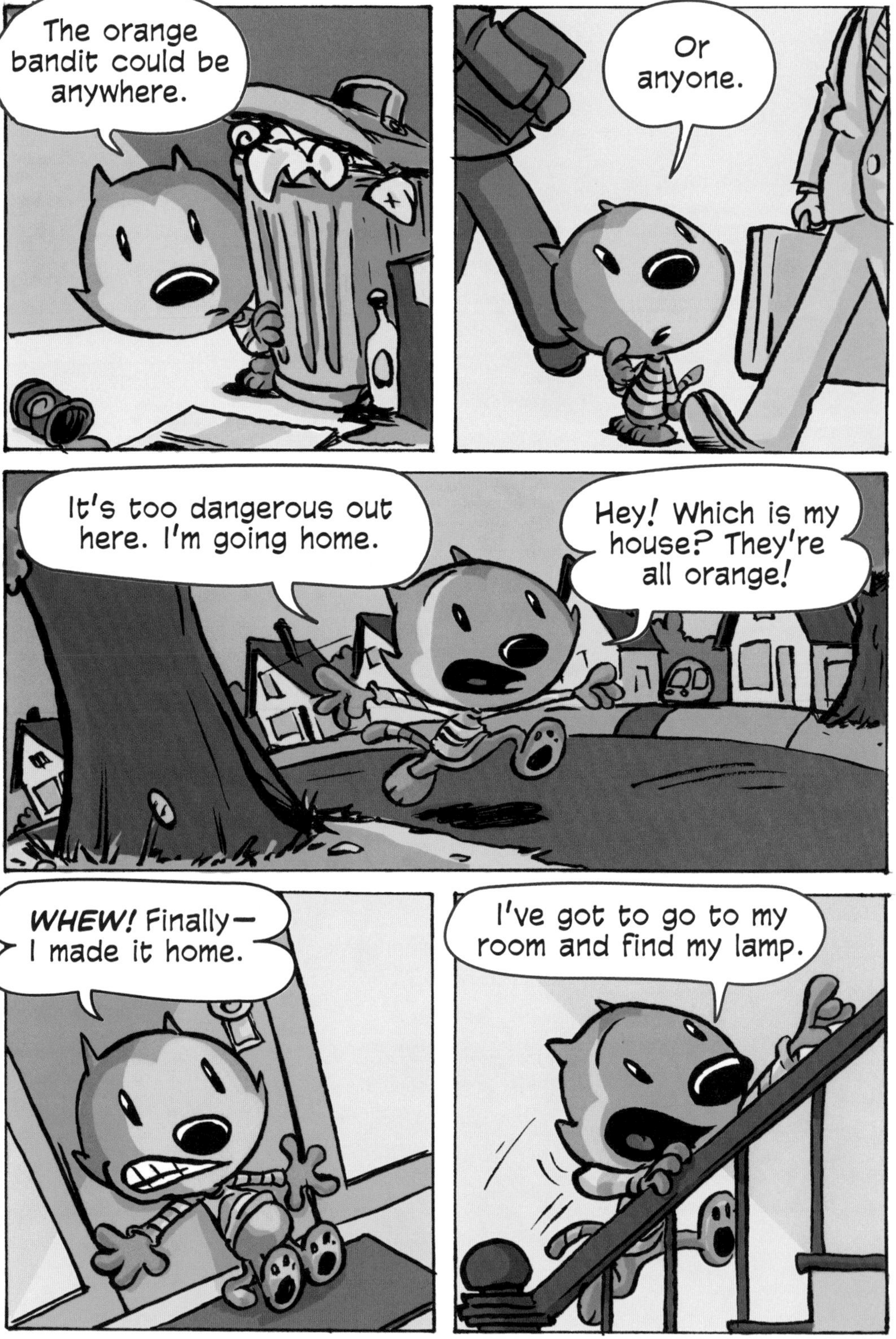
The orange bandit could be anywhere.
Or anyone.
It's too dangerous out here. I'm going home.
Hey! Which is my house? They're all orange!
WHEW! Finally—I made it home.
I've got to go to my room and find my lamp.

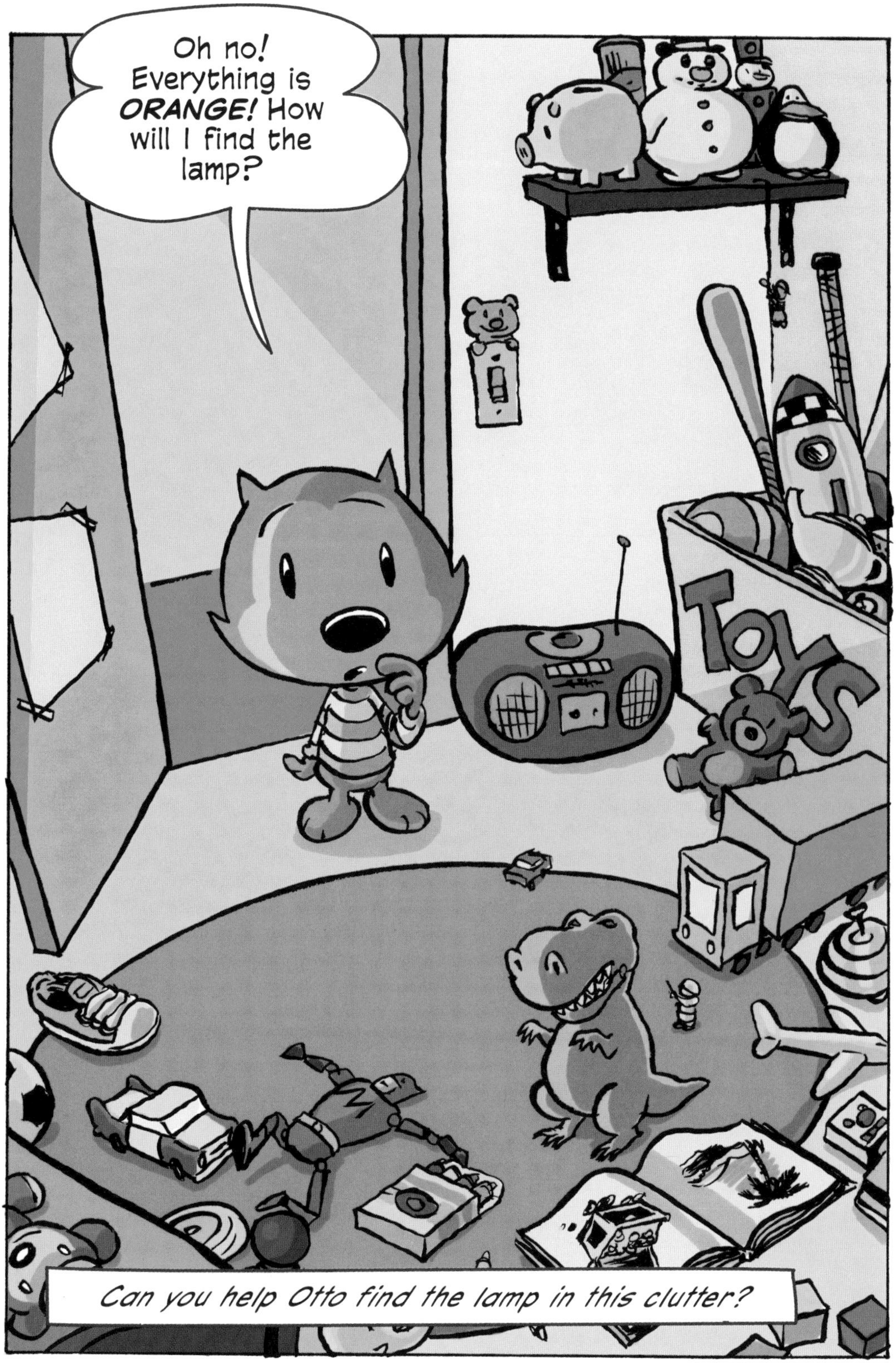
Oh no! Everything is ORANGE! How will I find the lamp?
TOYS
Can you help Otto find the lamp in this clutter?

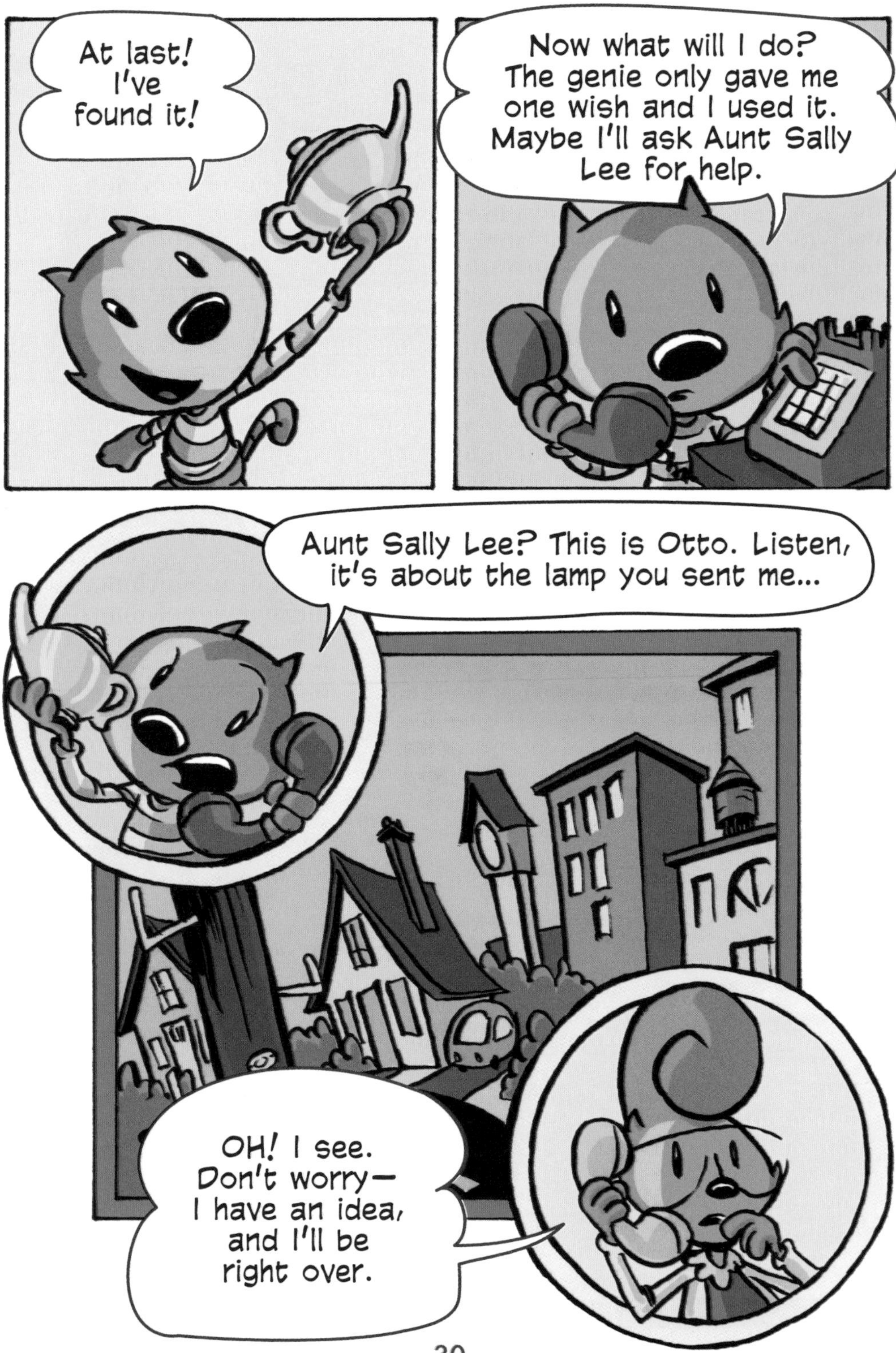
At last! I've found it!
Now what will I do? The genie only gave me one wish and I used it. Maybe I'll ask Aunt Sally Lee for help.
Aunt Sally Lee? This is Otto. Listen, it's about the lamp you sent me...
OH! I see. Don't worry— I have an idea, and I'll be right over.

CHAPTER THREE:

A NEW WISH

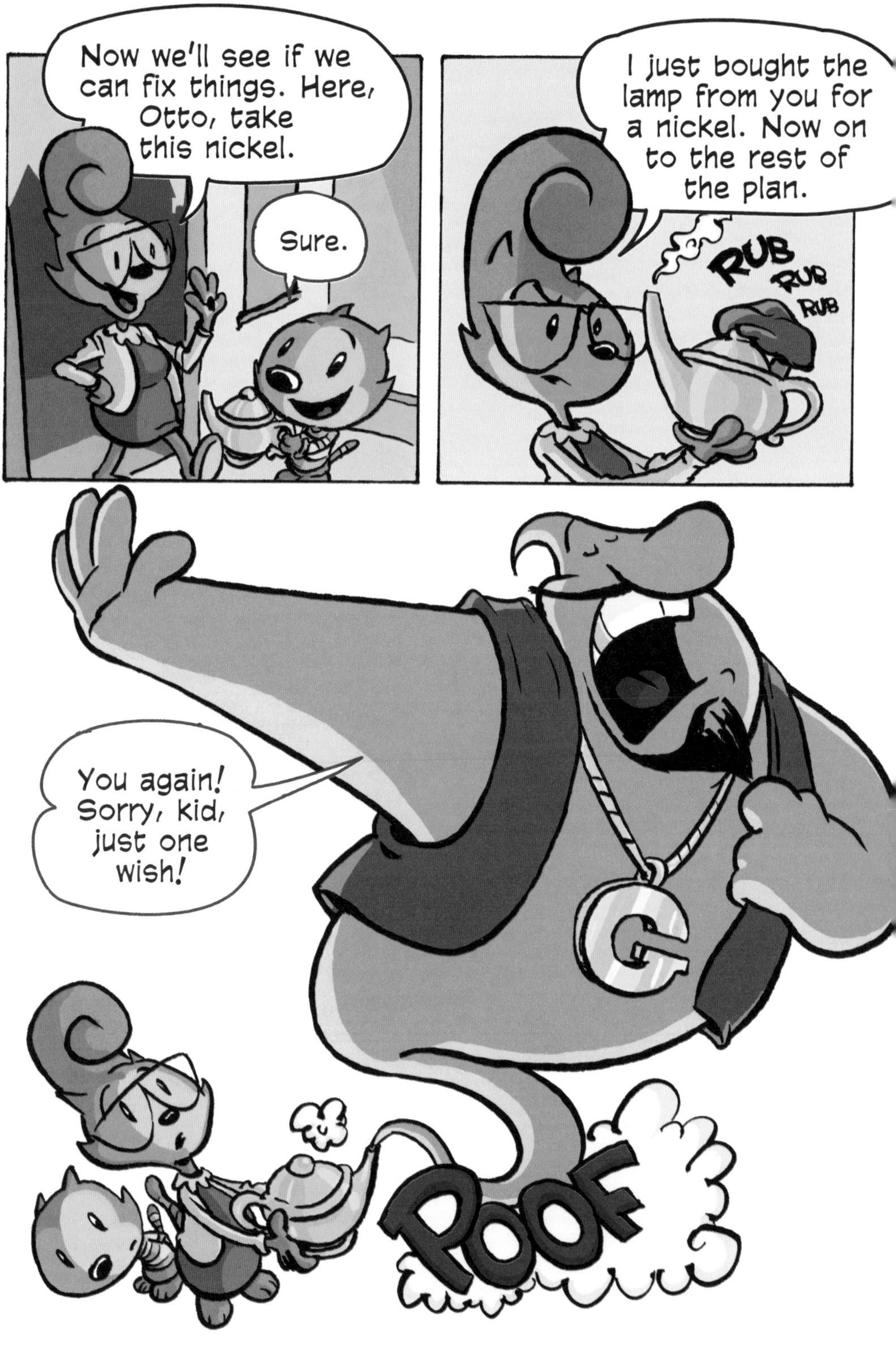

Now we'll see if we can fix things. Here, Otto, take this nickel.
Sure.
I just bought the lamp from you for a nickel. Now on to the rest of the plan.
RUB RUB RUB
You again! Sorry, kid, just one wish!
POOF

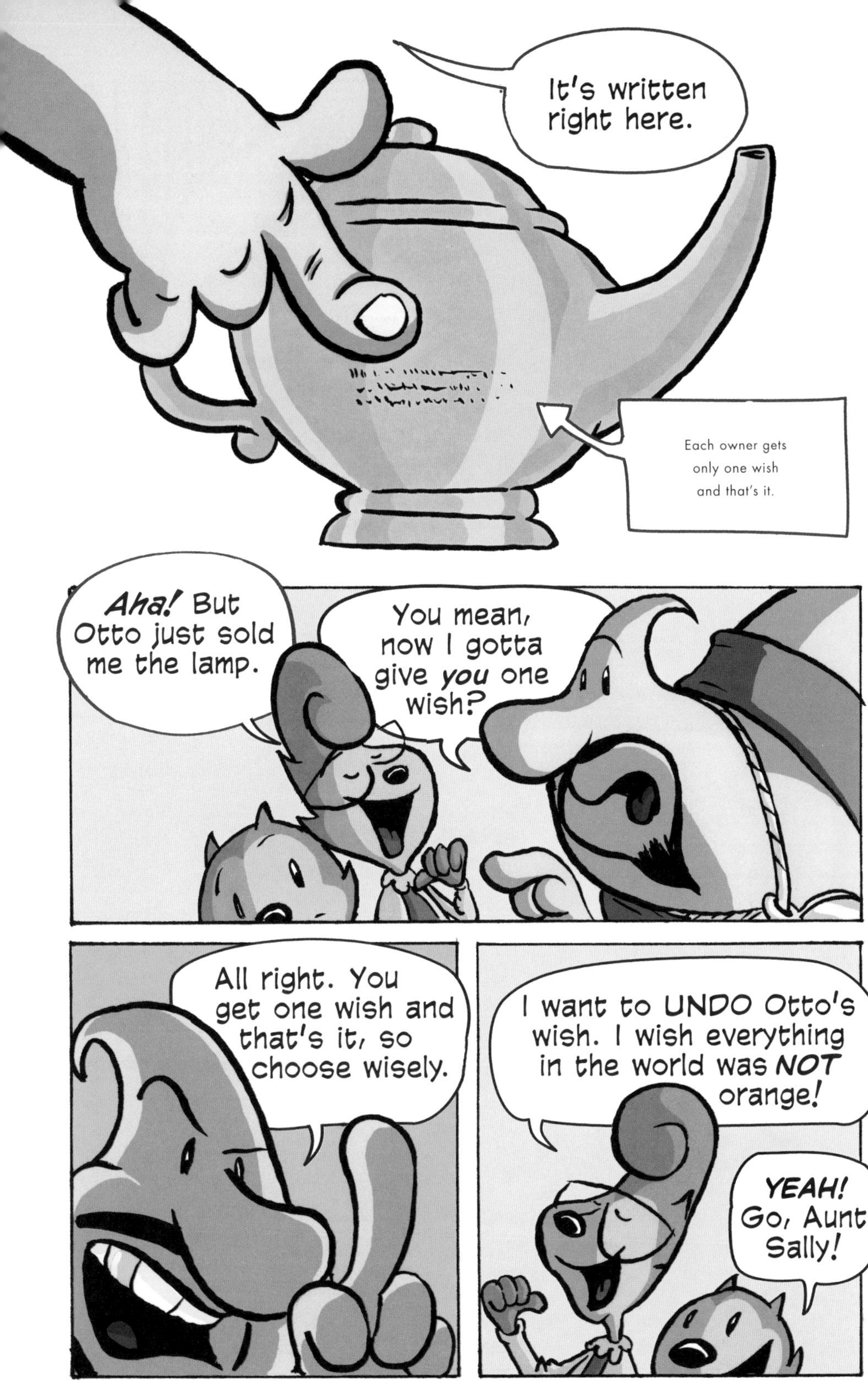
It's written right here.
Each owner gets only one wish and that's it.
Aha! But Otto just sold me the lamp.
You mean, now I gotta give *you* one wish?
All right. You get one wish and that's it, so choose wisely.
I want to UNDO Otto's wish. I wish everything in the world was *NOT* orange!
YEAH! Go, Aunt Sally!

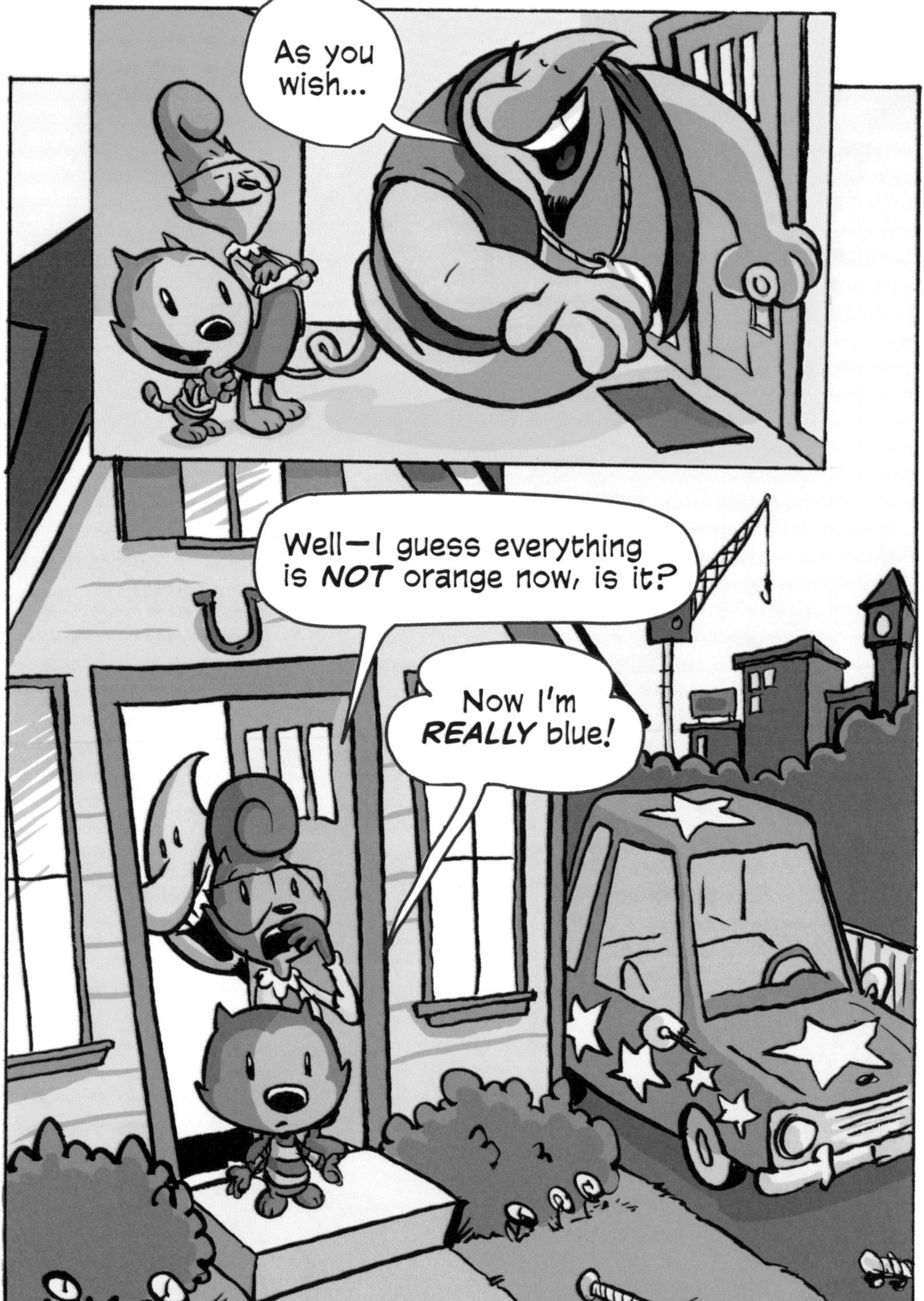
As you wish...
Well—I guess everything is NOT orange now, is it?
Now I'm REALLY blue!

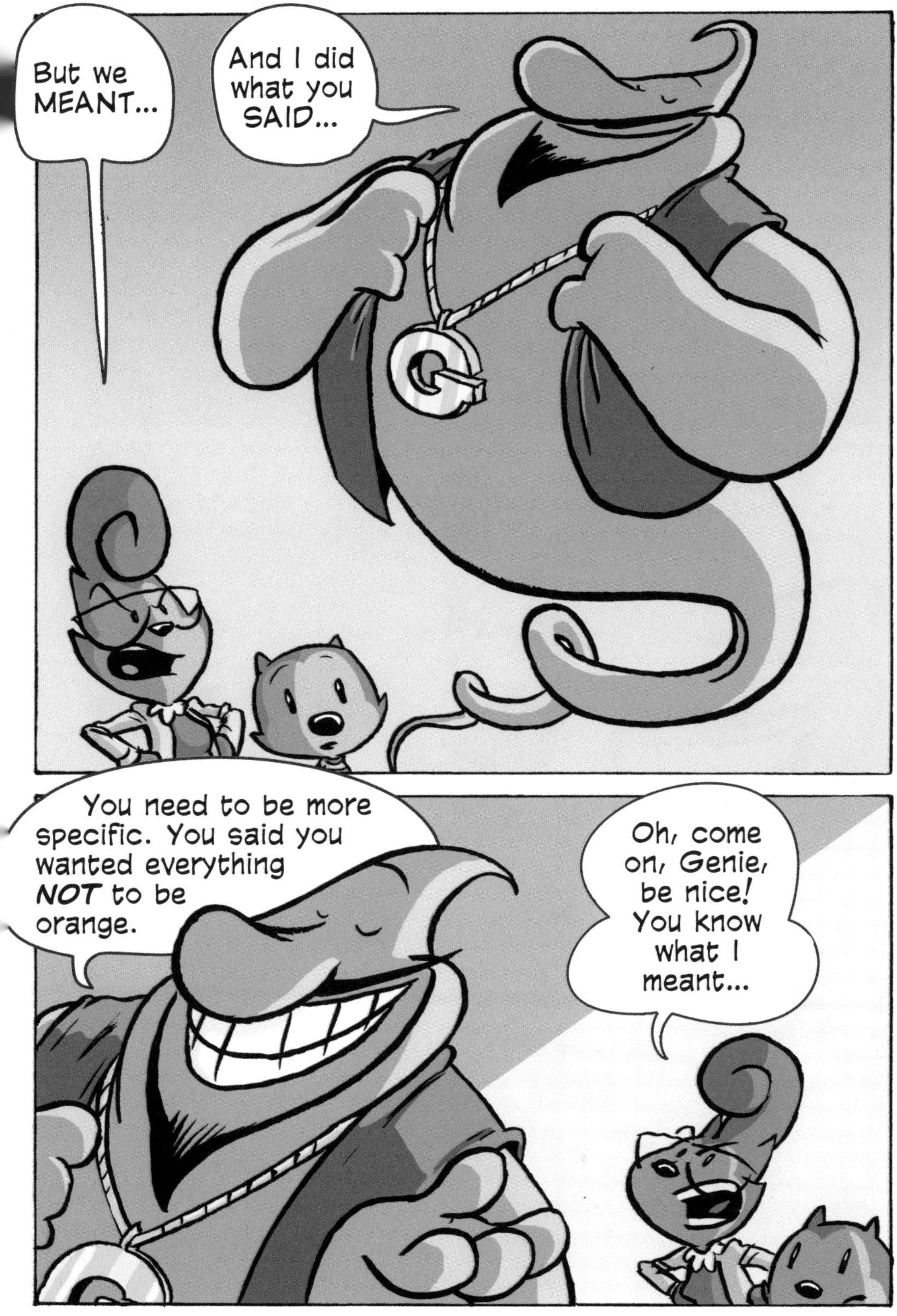
But we MEANT...
And I did what you SAID...
You need to be more specific. You said you wanted everything ***NOT*** to be orange.
Oh, come on, Genie, be nice! You know what I meant...

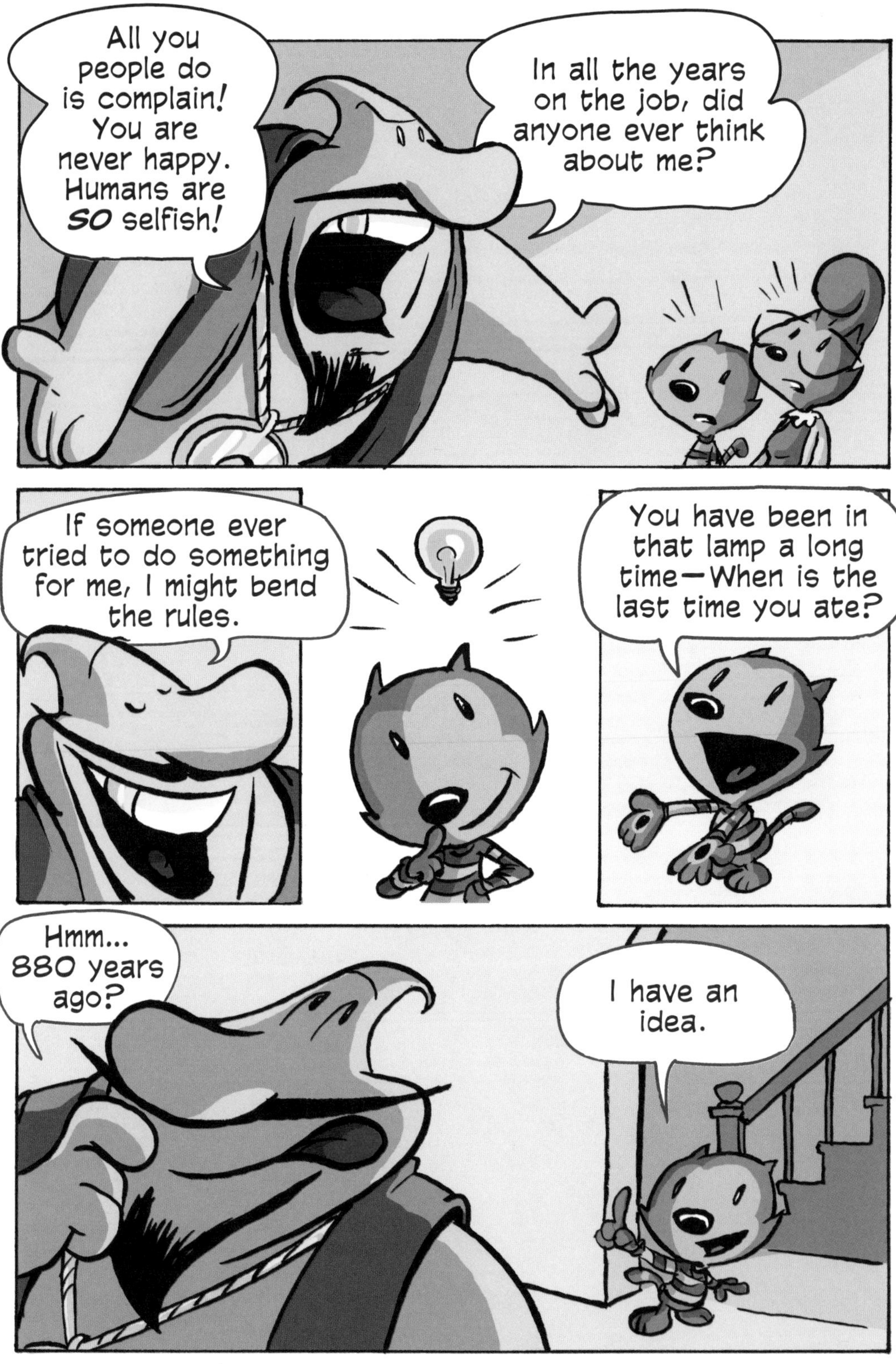
All you people do is complain! You are never happy. Humans are *SO* selfish!
In all the years on the job, did anyone ever think about me?
If someone ever tried to do something for me, I might bend the rules.
You have been in that lamp a long time—When is the last time you ate?
Hmm... 880 years ago?
I have an idea.

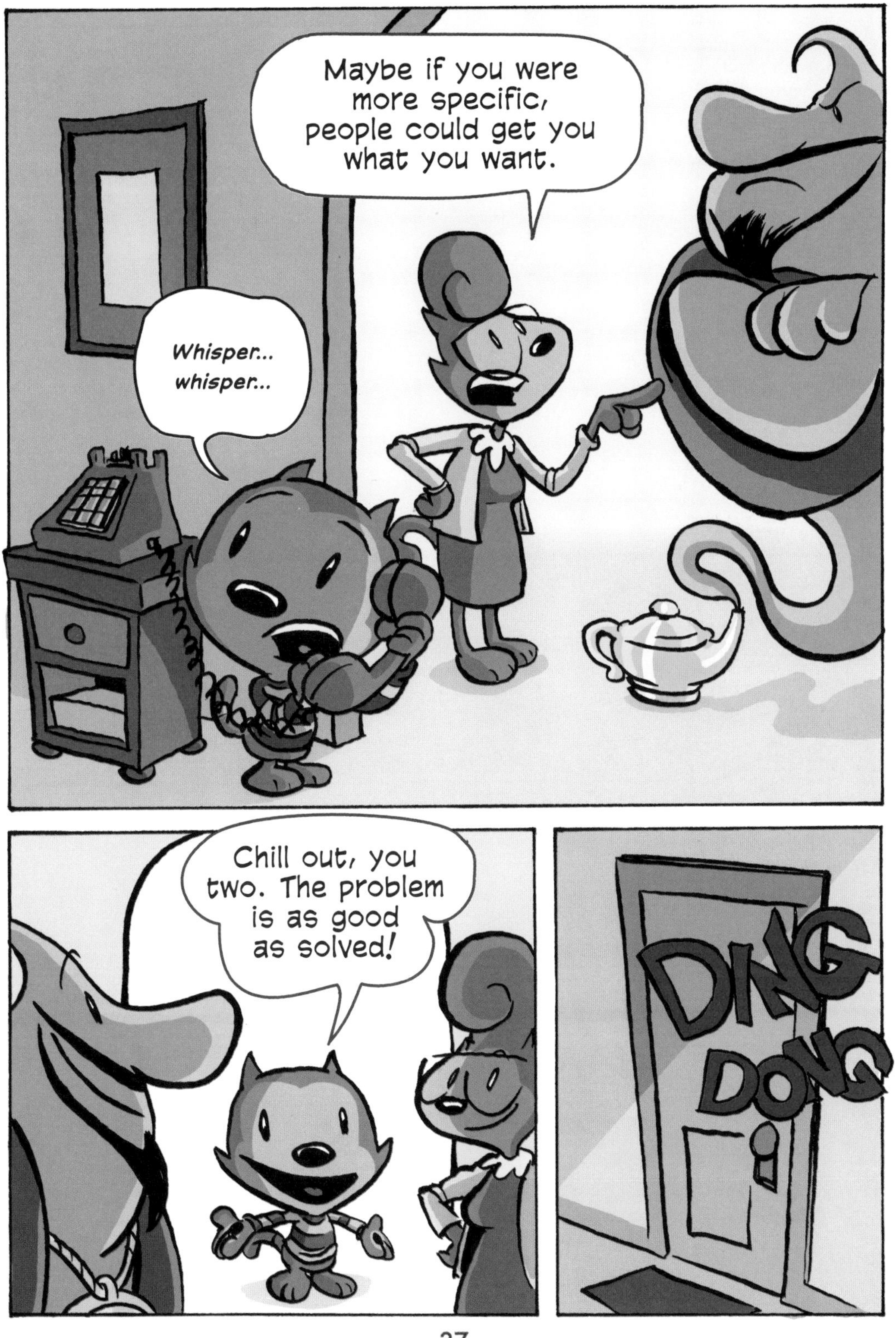
Maybe if you were more specific, people could get you what you want.
Whisper... whisper...
Chill out, you two. The problem is as good as solved!
DING DONG

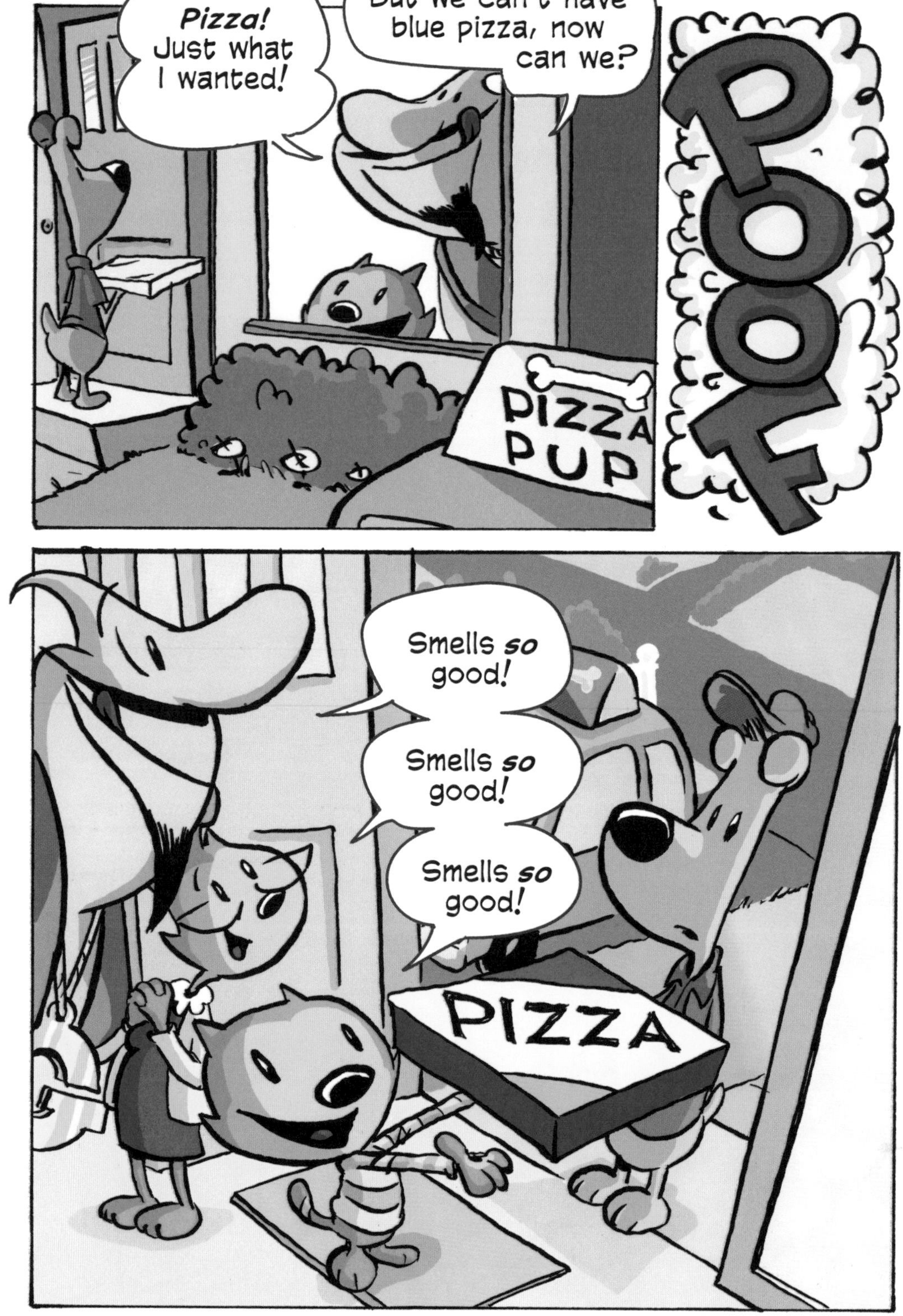
Pizza! Just what I wanted!
But we can't have blue pizza, now can we?
POOF
PIZZA PUP
Smells *so* good!
Smells *so* good!
Smells *so* good!
PIZZA

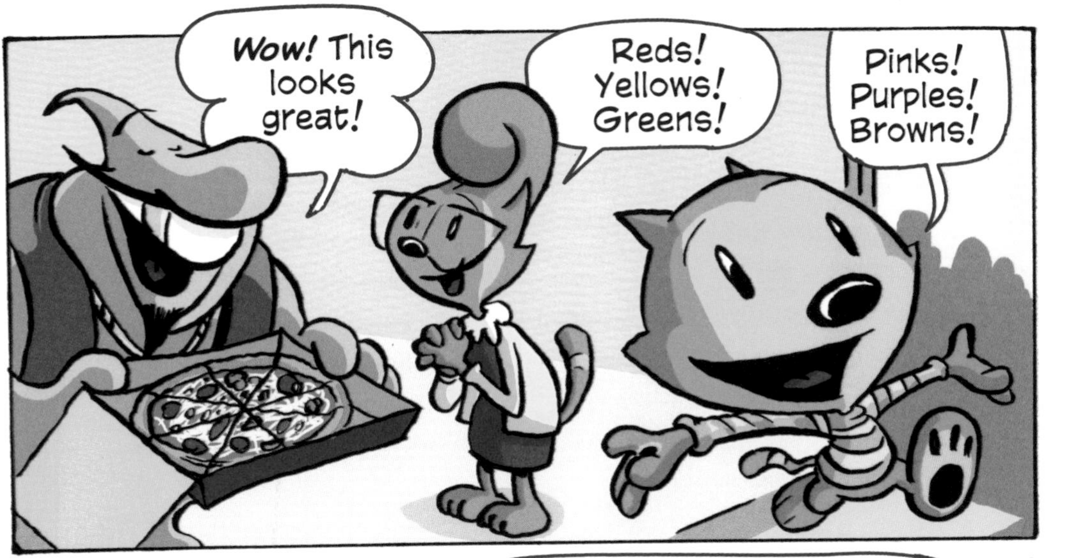

Wow! This looks great!
Reds! Yellows! Greens!
Pinks! Purples! Browns!

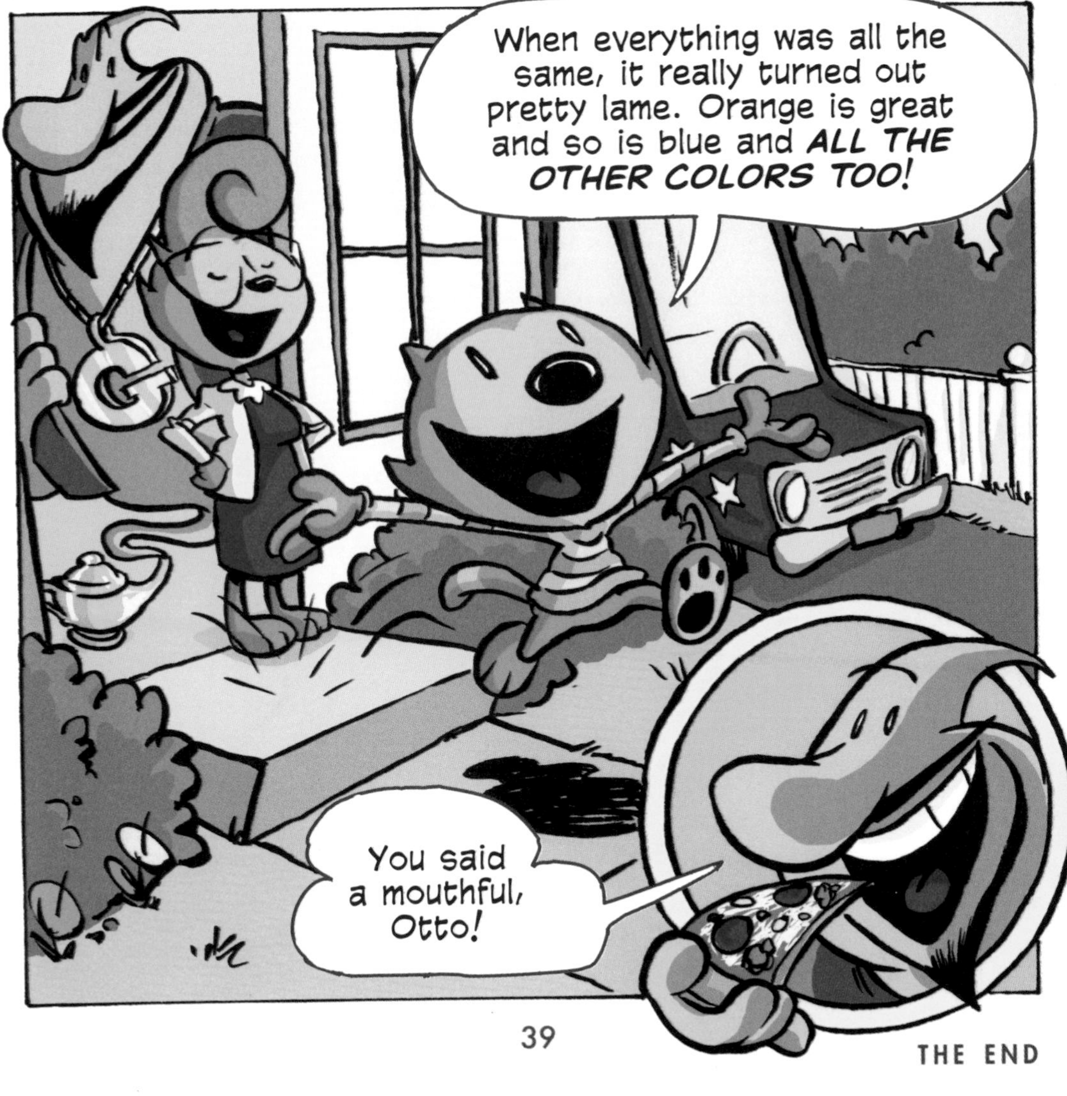

When everything was all the same, it really turned out pretty lame. Orange is great and so is blue and ALL THE OTHER COLORS TOO!
You said a mouthful, Otto!

THE END

TIPS FOR PARENTS AND TEACHERS:
HOW TO READ
COMICS WITH

DATE D

Kids **love**

make the

let both emerging and relucta

vocabulary. But since comics

reading them with kids:

GUIDE YOUNG READ

text, but keep it at the

the very important facial exp.

HAM IT UP! Think of the comic book story

read with expression and intonation. Assign parts o.

sound effects, a great way to reinforce phonics skills.

LET THEM GUESS. Comics provide lots of context for the words, so

emerging readers can make informed guesses. Like jigsaw puzzles,

comics ask readers to make connections, so check a young audience's

understanding by asking, "What's this character thinking?" (but don't be

surprised if a kid finds some of the comics' subtle details faster than you).

TALK ABOUT THE PICTURES. Point out how the artist paces the story with

pauses (silent panels) or speeded-up action (a burst of short panels). Discuss how

the size and shape of the panels carry meaning.

ABOVE ALL, ENJOY! There is of course never one right way to read,

so go for the shared pleasure. Once children make the story happen in

their imagination, they have discovered the thrill of reading, and you

won't be able to stop them. At that point, just go get them more books,

and more comics.

TOON-BOOKS.com

SEE OUR FREE ONLINE CARTOON MAKERS,
LESSON PLANS, AND MUCH MORE.